"I'm not the romantic type."

Rea's murmur was barely audible. "Aren't you, Rea?" Burke was still smiling. "Perhaps that's just as well, considering you're about to make a quite unromantic marriage."

She twisted her hands together in her lap. Talk of this marriage still brought her heart into her throat. There would be lies, deception…and she shrank from it. "How will you explain us?" she asked.

"The situation will explain itself, I think, Rea. My grandfather will get what he's always wanted, a grandson; and I shall cease to be regarded in the county as a likely candidate for the marriage stakes."

He shot a grin at her. "And you, my child, acquire freedom from drudgery. In my opinion, the few necessary lies we'll be obliged to tell will be well worth it."

Harlequin Presents Collection

A new series... of old favorites!

Harlequin has been publishing its widely read *Presents* series for more than eight years. These beautiful romance novels, written by the world's most popular authors of romantic fiction, have become the No. 1 best-selling love stories in more than eighty countries.

Now we are pleased to make available to you, our more recent readers, a chance to enjoy many of the early *Presents* favorites you may have missed.

We know you'll enjoy these carefully selected volumes. They come from our not-too-distant past—a past we are proud of, a past we are sure you'll love!

VIOLET
WINSPEAR

wife without kisses

Originally published as Harlequin Presents #9

Harlequin Books

TORONTO • LONDON • LOS ANGELES • AMSTERDAM
SYDNEY • HAMBURG • PARIS • STOCKHOLM • ATHENS • TOKYO

Harlequin Presents edition published June 1973
ISBN 0-373-15001-6

Second printing June 1973
Third printing July 1973
Fourth printing August 1973
Fifth printing November 1973
Sixth printing July 1974
Seventh printing August 1974
Eighth printing April 1976
Ninth printing June 1976
Tenth printing September 1976
Eleventh printing February 1977
Twelfth printing March 1977
Thirteenth printing March 1979

This *Harlequin Presents Collection* edition
published September 1980

Original hardcover edition published in 1961
by Mills & Boon Limited

Printed in Canada

CHAPTER ONE

IT was one of those self-consciously smart seaside hotels, with doors that swung with a flourish, spotless napery and cutlery on the dining-room tables and a wasp-waisted clerk at the reception desk.

Rea, as she shifted Mrs. Damien's jewel-case from her right hand to her left, rather tiredly reflected that these hotels all looked and felt and smelled alike. How much more interesting life would be if Mrs. Damien chose, just once, to stay in a crofter's cottage, or on a boathouse, or at some quaint old inn, with dormer windows under thatch!

Imagination Laura Damien might have—was she not the incredible producer of twenty-nine romantic best-sellers?—but Rea was continually astounded that such a fertile and romantic imagination had its being in such a gross and comfort-greedy body.

With a buccaneer flourish of her wrist Laura signed the register and then stared boldly into the pettish face of the clerk. "Anybody important stopping here?" she demanded, pushing the register towards Rea, who took up the pen and bent to sign her name, one eye marking the clerk's goggle-eyed reaction not only to Laura's effrontery, but to the heavy make-up adorning her face, the enormous fur collar enclosing her throat, the absolute self-assurance of the absolutely self-satisfied that stared out of her eyes.

But before he had time to reply to her question, she had swung round from the reception desk and was staring at a man who had just entered the hotel and was sauntering towards the lift, a cigarette between his lips and a raincoat thrown over his shoulder.

"My God!" Rea heard her say, then she was plunging towards the lift in the patent leather shoes that always seemed too small for her, calling out: "Burke! Burke Ryeland!"

He heard her and turned from the lift, taking his cigarette from his mouth. Rea, following somewhat tentatively in Laura's wake, saw his very black brows pull together in a quick frown as he contemplated the stout exuberance of the advancing Laura Damien, her large, scarlet-tipped hands outstretched towards him, her eyes, the crude blue that amateur artists always seem to paint their skies and their seas, raking him from head to foot as she exclaimed: "My dear boy, I thought you were dead!" She clutched his arms and shook him. "We all thought you were dead. Dead and buried in that awful Peruvian jungle you went to explore."

He stared at her, patently trying to place her. She saw this and burst out laughing. "Maybe I've put on some weight, dear boy, but surely you remember Laura Damien? I was always at those house-parties of Shaw Lacey's, at Richmond. Those crazy house-parties! With Shaw, the funny boy, spouting D. H. Lawrence, and his wife, Letty, dancing in a scarlet shawl on the grand piano. Remember?" Again she shook his arms. "You must remember!"

"Of course—Shaw Lacey—and Letty!" Amazed recollection had jumped into his eyes. "Unabridged Lawrence for supper and tired turkey sandwiches for breakfast!" His dark, rather aloof face broke into a slight smile. "We were all a bit batty in those days, weren't we?"

Laura nodded, a sudden look of nostalgia wiping some of the bold worldliness from her face. "Six—seven years ago, it must be," she said. She stared up into Burke Ryeland's face, her glance sharpening to curiosity. "I'm sure I read somewhere that you were lost in Peru."

"I was." He spoke crisply. Then his glance swung away from Laura and settled on the hesitant Rea, a red leather jewel-case clutched in one hand, a plaid travelling rug over her arm, her very obvious youth and her thin, coltish legs thrown into sharp relief by the buxom hardness of Laura. Burke Ryeland's frown returned and he pinned Rea's wavering glance with his own, held it forcibly, until Laura drawled: "This is my little Rea Glyn, dear boy. She pounds my terrible typewriter for me. I couldn't possibly do it. The thing would jam and slip and do all sorts of unbearable things and drive me quite crazy." She won Burke's glance back to her and gaily showed him two perfect rows of very white teeth. "Are you still writing those incredibly clever travel books of yours, Burke?"

He shook his head and she pulled a mouth of exaggerated dismay. "Look," she patted his sleeve, "let's have dinner together. I must hear about Peru. I'm sure you had some very exciting adventures—and I want to hear how you came to get lost."

But the suggestion wasn't received with enthusiasm. He withdrew his arm from the clutch of her scarlet nails and rang for the lift. "Sorry," he said, "but I'm dining out tonight."

"Tomorrow, then?" A coquettish pleading sat oddly on her large-featured face. "For old times' sake, dear boy?"

He stared back at her, moodily. "I'm not particularly interested in old times, Mrs. Damien. They hold no charm for me." He turned, then, hearing the heavy whirr of the lift, and as it settled to a standstill and the doors slid open, he stepped into the lighted interior of it without a backward glance.

Laura Damien watched its swift ascent and Rea saw the quick irritated blood flow under the paint upon her cheeks. "He had no need to be that rude!" she exclaimed, jerking at the fur collar of her coat. "But then he was always an insolent, take-me-or-leave-me sort of animal." Her eyes met Rea's. "Get the keys," she snapped. "I want to have a lie-down before dinner, my head is simply splitting after that train journey."

Laura had booked a suite for herself and a single room for Rea, and as Rea unpacked her suitcase, her eyes kept stealing to the window, which overlooked the Hastings promenade. Though a slight drizzle had arrived, throwing a mist along the sea front and over the pier, Rea knew a sudden longing to be out in it, to be free of this hothouse of an hotel and the depressing thought of yet another evening spent eating with Laura, of playing cards with Laura, of being submerged in the incessant conversation of Laura.

She drew a fierce little sigh. To be independent of employment! To have money enough to go anywhere one wished; to go as far as China or Siam. Or maybe Peru.

Rea drew a finger down the steamy glass of the window, wondering a little to herself. Then her reflections were abruptly cut short, for the door of her room flew open and Laura marched in, an orange negligée swinging back from her thick, bare legs and an expression of exaggerated suffering on her face.

"Darling," she burst out, "have you any aspirin? My head is killing me and I haven't a thing to take."

Rea went to the dressing-table and searched her handbag, but the only thing medicinal it contained was a small tin of adhesive tape.

"Shall I go out and get you some aspirin?" she asked. Laura nodded, too absorbed in a self-pitying fondling of her aching brows to remember that Rea could have bought aspirin at the reception desk downstairs. "If you will, darling. I can't possibly stand this damned pounding much longer." She drifted away and Rea quickly snatched up her coat, took her purse from her handbag and sped along the corridor to the stairs. She raced down them like a boy, her long legs flashing under her flared skirt, her fair fringe dancing above her hazel eyes. She looked more like sixteen than nineteen in her excitement at having escaped the hotel for a few precious minutes.

She met the cold sting of the rain with a smile. It smelled good. It smelled of the sea. She strode along, her hands thrust into the pockets of her coat, glad of this chance to stretch her legs, cramped after the train journey from London.

Laura was funny. They had been in the middle of *Autumn Affair* when she had suddenly announced that the story was dull, that she felt dull, and that a short spell at the seaside might refresh her brain. "We'll take the portable, in case I get a few new ideas," she had said. "We'll go to Hastings. It used to be quite a haunt of mine when I was younger. So quaint, darling."

Rea located a chemist's shop and bought a large bottle of aspirin tablets. Then she made her way back to the hotel, noticing the long, silver-grey racer that stood in the kerb, sleek and dangerous-looking and gaily upholstered in red leather. She was so busy looking at it, wondering what it would be like to ride in such a car, tearing into the face of the wind, that she walked straight into a man emerging from the hotel. As she gasped and almost fell, he reached out a large hand, steadying her. "Watch yourself, Rea Glyn," he murmured, and for a speeding second Rea looked into eyes of that startling, electric blue seen only at the edge of a fierce flame. Then his hand released her and he was striding to the kerb and climbing behind the wheel of that gleaming grey car.

Rea's eyes were large as she watched it dart out from the kerb and rapidly disappear into the rain and gloom of fast-approaching evening.

The aspirins did the trick, and Laura's headache had quite abated by the time she and Rea went down to dinner.

She swept into the crowded dining-room, resplendent in moss-green silk, a great knot of pearls bouncing on her bosom and an opal the size of a penny glistening on her right index finger. As she followed the waiter to a table, she cast bold eyes over the assembled diners, aware of causing a mild sensation and frankly revelling in the fact. She took up the menu with a flourish and remarked to Rea: "I feel a little abandoned tonight, darling, in a sportive mood—and that calls for champagne."

She then proceeded to order champagne, while Rea marked the interested way a moustached and immaculate diner at the next table was studying Laura, chewing his dinner in a reflective manner and obviously trying to decide whether she was someone's wealthy widow or an actress from the local repertory theatre. Rea smiled to herself, and Laura, catching the smile, queried a trifle sarcastically: "Are you sitting on a feather?"

Rea's smile deepened. "I just feel rather happy," she said. "I think I like Hastings."

Laura looked blasé. "Quaint child, aren't you?" she drawled, and her blue eyes travelled slowly round the dining-room, obviously searching for someone. "I suppose he did go out," she murmured at last. "I wonder why he's playing hard to know?"

"Burke Ryeland?" Rea asked, knowing full well that Laura meant the mysterious Burke Ryeland.

"Who else?" Laura snorted. Then a rather inquisitive gleam stole into her eyes. "What did you make of him?"

Rea floundered for an answer. She didn't really know what she had made of the man, except that he had a nice car and a rather nice speaking voice.

"Did you think him attractive?" Laura demanded.

"More forceful than merely attractive, I think," Rea replied.

"Forceful, eh?" Laura's painted eyebrows arched in an impudent fashion. "Attractive, too, dear, take it from me. He was always that. Letty Lacey, in the good old bad days, was crazy about him. It was a good job that silly boy of a husband of hers never knew—he'd have put a bullet through Burke. Not that I believe anything really *risqué* went on between Letty and Burke. There was at that time, if I remember rightly, a bit of a wild young ballet-dancer in his life." Laura's brows drew together. "I wonder what came of that affair? And I wonder what the devil he's doing here in Hastings? It's hardly his sort of stamping ground, when you come to think of some of the out-of-the-way places he's visited. Peru, now!" She tapped a reflective scarlet finger-nail against her chin. "Something mighty funny happened there, you could tell that from the way he didn't want to talk about the place."

"To tell you the truth," Rea admitted, "I thought Burke Ryeland a rather supercilious sort of person."

"Why shouldn't he be?" Laura smiled as she refilled her wine glass. "His family is one of the richest and oldest in England. His grandfather's house in Somerset is a showpiece. Have you never heard of King's Beeches?"

Rea shook her head.

"King's Beeches, my dear," Laura said, a hint of reverence creeping into her voice, "is considered one of the landmarks of Somerset—on a par with the Cheddar Gorge, almost. I'm surprised you haven't heard of it, or seen a photograph of it."

"Well, I haven't." Rea spoke diffidently, rather annoyed by Laura's cool assumption that she had been impressed by the very self-assured Burke Ryeland. Just because Laura had such an intense interest in men—and they were always very much younger than herself, Rea had noticed—she seemed to think it unnatural to the point of sheer freakishness in Rea that she found them quite unexciting. Several times Laura had conspired to throw her alone with one of her youthful literary friends, and Rea had not enjoyed the experience. She had nothing to say to these smart, cynical young men, and she knew they laughed about her behind her back. She had overheard herself described by one of them as "that funny little elf with the nun-complex."

Her lips were tremulous against the rim of her wine glass and a little flare of temper shot up inside her. Let Laura and her friends think her funny! Let them! Her father had once said to her: "The most important thing in life, my dear, is to be always true unto yourself. Be that rigorously, my darling. Don't join all the other sheep, doing this and doing that because it is the fashion, or because they laugh at you for being outside the fashion. Snap your fingers and tread your own path, always."

Rea, remembering those quiet words, was reassured. She glanced across the table at Laura, bold in her green silk, loungingly at ease as she lit a cigarette. So sure of herself! And it wasn't success alone made her that way. It was something inherent in her. She could never have been pretty, not even as a girl, yet she was undeniably popular with the many young men she gathered around her. It was a kind of power, Rea decided; something that went beyond the face, the body—even age. . . .

"Stop staring at me," Laura suddenly growled, cigarette smoke jetting from her nostrils. "Those great big nun's eyes of yours give me the willies. What are you trying to find with them—my soul?" Then she laughed. "I have too big a bank balance to possess a soul, my sweet."

"You're very cynical, aren't you?" Rea remarked.

"One has to be," Laura replied, looking amused. "It's modern armour, my dear. This is a big, cruel world and one has to be born tough, or learn to be tough, in order to come out on top of it. Take Burke Ryeland!" She waved cigarette smoke away from her face. "That laddie is as hard as slate. Attractive, enormously rich, and very charming when he's in the mood to be—but I don't imagine he's ever cared a darn for anyone in his entire life. Even the little ballet girl he used to run around with was, I strongly suspect, a mere piece of pretty distraction for him in between his bouts of equatorial wandering. I never heard that anything permanent came of the affair. She was crazy about him, of course, but he had a sort of—of arrogant coolness in his attitude towards her—and to all women, come to that. An 'I'll-notice-you-when-it-suits-me-to' sort of attitude. But when a man is as attractive as he is, and as well off, women accept the arrogance; they even seem to revel in it."

Laura's laugh came softly, while her eyes grew mocking as they watched Rea. "But you wouldn't understand that, would you, my dear?" she said.

Rea shook an emphatic head. "I think they must be crazy," she exclaimed. "Picked up and petted, just like kittens, and then carelessly dropped back on the floor!"

Laura laughed lazily. "How quaint you are, darling," she drawled. "Wouldn't you like to be picked up and petted by Burke Ryeland?" Her eyes, through the wreathing cigarette smoke, were openly malicious. "Or would you scratch him? Tear that lean, brown cheek with your naughty little nails?"

"Oh, really, Mrs. Damien!" Rea looked confused and exasperated together.

"Oh, really, Miss Glyn!" Then Laura shrugged. "But Burke isn't very likely to want to pick you up and pet you, baby face, so you can stop looking apprehensive.

You're hardly his type, unless those steaming Peruvian forests have thinned his blood."

Laura's eyes swept the untouched, unawakened face of the girl opposite, and she knew an impatient contempt. "No, he wouldn't be very likely to look at you—you've never been kissed, have you?"

Rea flushed hotly. She hated, despised these conversations, Laura's ever-present curiosity about her. "No, I don't go in for promiscuous kissing," she shot back.

"Saving yourself for the right man, huh?" Laura laughed huskily. "Looking at a man won't tell you he's the right one, honey. You've got to get a lot closer than that before you'll know."

CHAPTER TWO

THE following morning, as though put upon her mettle by the remarkable amount of champagne she had consumed the evening before, Laura informed Rea at breakfast that she had decided to scrap six whole chapters of *Autumn Affair* and to write them afresh.

She tossed a bundle of scribbling across the table, saying with a complacent smile: "I've been at work since five-thirty and my wrist is just about killing me. You can start typing that little lot out as soon as you've finished breakfast."

"Yes, Mrs. Damien." Rea glanced at the bundle of notes and her heart, never too full of hope, dismissed its plans for an exploration of Hastings. If Laura's dull mood had evaporated to this extent, that she took her fountain pen to paper at half-past five in the morning, the green portable, with its rows of white keys, would be all the scenery she, Rea, would see for quite a few days to come.

Which surmise proved a correct one.

For the next six long days Rea was kept busy feeding the insatiable portable with yards of quarto paper, while her slender, mobile fingers hammered out an incessant bombardment of words. The rain that had seen their arrival on the Sunday departed in a gay flood of sunshine and the historical little town beyond the hotel windows turned so warm and inviting that there were moments when Rea's fingers grew very, very rebellious on the keys of the portable.

It wasn't until the Saturday evening that a blear-eyed, wrist-sore Rea won her release from the dancing keys that earned her bread for her.

She made her way to the pier.

All day the September sun had shone brightly and there was still a fairly large crowd out upon the pier, stretched in deckchairs, lounging at the railings, and wandering in and out of the fun arcade and the restaurant.

Rea walked to the very end of the pier and stood at the railings, breathing deeply of the tangy air, grateful for the invigorating feel of it against her tired eyes and through her hair. There was noise and laughter all about her; the silky wash of the sea as it came in against the supports of the pier. There was, over everything, a gay warmth, a holiday release; something that quickened the blood and made of life, for these few precious moments, a gift to be held very closely, very lovingly.

"So you've finally escaped?" a low, pleasant voice suddenly murmured in her ear, while a small cloud of expensive cigarette smoke drifted piquant and sharp to her nostrils.

She stirred, dragging her tired eyes from the almost hypnotic dance of silver light on the slowly moving water. She stared at the large, lounging figure now at the rail beside her. "Mrs. Damien has been working like mad on her new book," she said. She watched Burke Ryeland through the gloom, startled and uneasy. There was about this man a lazy distinction: a cool, self-assured air that made her feel clumsily young—all feet and legs and straggly hair. Self-consciously she pushed her hair back from her face, her cheeks growing warm as he drawled: "Do you enjoy pounding Mrs. Damien's terrible typewriter?"

"She isn't a bad sort of person to work for," Rea replied, a trifle defensively.

"She reminds me of a boa-constrictor," he retorted, lazily, blowing his expensive cigarette smoke towards the sea, "wrapping her great painted self about you, Rea Glyn, and squeezing you dry of all youthful resilience. How long do you intend to be squeezed dry?"

"I—I don't understand you." Rea was bewildered by him, a little unnerved by the wide stretch of his shoulders above her, the enigmatic smile playing about his well-shaped mouth.

"How old are you?" he asked.

"Nineteen."

"That much?" He seemed surprised, his eyes travelling up and down her slender, boyish body in its rust wool suit, with a prim little white collar enclosing her throat, and a small butterfly brooch pinned above the slight lift of her left breast. "Does your mother know how hard you work for Laura Damien?" he demanded.

"I have no mother," she retorted primly.

"Nor a father?"

She bit her lip and turned from him. She was still feeling the loss of her father, and talking about him still hurt. "My father died nine months ago. He had a blood disease—there was nothing to be done for him."

"You sound as if you miss him very much." Burke Ryeland spoke with a quiet kindliness. "Have you been working for Laura Damien ever since?"

She nodded. "There was no money, you see. I—I was lucky to get such a good job, but I used to do a lot of typing for my father—he wrote articles for gardening journals in his spare time; he was an awfully good gardener—so I was fairly proficient. Anyway, Mrs. Damien seemed to think so."

"You consider you've been lucky, eh?" Burke Ryeland's drawl held a smile. "My word, you're easily pleased, Rea Glyn!"

"Beggars can't be choosers!" Rea retorted, again with a flash of defensiveness. "Anyway, I'm grateful to Mrs. Damien. A person in her position can afford to pick and choose and—and I think it was extremely kind-hearted of her to choose to employ me. My secretarial qualifications, nine months ago, were pretty thin."

"Oh, I think Madame Damien knew what she was doing," Burke Ryeland broke in, his drawl at its smoothest, his reflections at their most caustic as he watched Rea. This, he thought, was obviously a kid who would work morning, noon and night without a murmur of complaint, and that qualification would far outshine any others for Laura Damien. Laura Damien, unaltered from the old days; still brassy and predatory and mammothly unconcerned that she had worked this child, Rea, until her great child's eyes were ready to pop out of her head!

"I—I understand you were a friend of Mrs. Damien's," Rea said, with a touch of youthful dignity, making him smile.

"Let's say we were once passingly acquainted," he amended. "She's hardly an island I'd care to stay long on."

"That's a curious simile, Mr. Ryeland," Rea was moved to remark.

"Writers are curious people, my dear. Even those wearing the 'ex' label." He studied her through the gloom and she saw that his eyes were quizzical. "Have you no rebellion in your young soul, Rea Glyn?" he abruptly queried.

"I—I don't think so." She fingered the smooth metal of the rail where she stood—then, honesty prevailing in her, she burst out: "No, I do rebel. I do long to break my chains—but I have to eat."

"Bravo!" Now he smiled. "I'm glad you said that." Abruptly he tossed the remainder of his cigarette into the sea and straightened to his full six feet three. "Will you come and have dinner with me, Rea?" he invited.

"D-dinner?" Rea's eyes went large with surprise. "But—but Mrs. Damien is expecting me back."

"Mrs. Damien can go to the devil!" His large cool hands came to her shoulders and he drew her round from the pier railings. "You've earned a break from that booming, bedizened female, my child. She's had you shut up in that damn hothouse of an hotel all the week."

"Well, I've been working," Rea protested.

"And now the working week is over and it's time to play. Come on." He grasped her hand and firmly led her from the pier, striding so freely that she had to run to keep up with him. When they reached his car, waiting sleekly in the kerb, he handed her in with a smile. "You can stop looking apprehensive," he commanded, climbing in beside her and leaning forward to switch on the ignition. "I assure you I'm no bold seducer of shy young things. I outgrew that tendency years ago."

The car shot out from the kerb and Rea stole a tentative, rather puzzled glance at Burke Ryeland's hard, fine profile. She was profoundly startled that he should approach her and ask her to dine with him; he hadn't struck her as a particularly sociable sort of person.

And from one or two remarks Laura Damien had let drop through the week, he had evidently been stringently avoiding her. A slight smile gleamed in Rea's eyes. The complacent Laura would hardly feel flattered if she knew that her dull little typist had achieved the dinner invitation she had desired so strongly herself. She'd be as astounded by it as Rea was.

Her eyes dwelt on the slight feathering of silver at Burke Ryeland's temple and she found herself wondering how old he might be. Possibly thirty-six or seven, she decided; surely no more?

The sleek grey car headed into St. Leonard's and in about a quarter of an hour drew in before a quiet-looking restaurant down a side turning. They suddenly seemed cut off from the noisy holiday crowds and as Burke ushered Rea into the restaurant, the quiet charm and elegance of the place abruptly shocked her awake to the fact that this was one of those deceptively modest-looking places, catering for a moneyed and selective clientele. She drew back in alarm against Burke's arm. "I'm—I'm not dressed for this!" she gasped.

"Let me be the judge of that," he retorted, and propelled her to a table, to which a waiter came at once, murmuring a deferential good evening and handing Burke a menu.

Burke opened it, his eyes upon Rea. "I hope all that hard work of yours has made you hungry," he said. "The food here is very good." His eyes scanned the menu. "Do you like lobster?" he asked.

Her head gave a nervous little jerk and he grinned slightly as he turned to the waiter. "We'll follow a light soup with the lobster mayonnaise, I think. Then breast of partridges, with foie gras, truffles and soufflé potatoes."

The waiter inclined his deferential head and departed, and while Burke awaited the wine-waiter, he sat back to regard Rea with amused eyes. Her fair hair was tossed from their ride and she was self-consciously smoothing it back, her eyes travelled round the restaurant and taking rather awed note of its quietly distinctive décor and its quietly elegant diners.

"You look perfectly presentable, my dear girl, so do stop fussing," Burke murmured.

Rea met his smiling eyes across the table, bringing her hand down from her hair. She sat up prim and straight in her chair. "Mrs. Damien doesn't eat in this kind of place," she said.

"I'm not Mrs. Damien!" he retorted crisply.

A grin jumped about Rea's mouth. "She'd have a fit, you know, if she knew I was with you."

"Why?"

"She—she thinks I'm scared of men."

"Well, you are, aren't you?" His black brows rose quizzically above the piercing blue of his eyes. "Aren't you a little weak at the knees right this very moment?"

The laughter in his eyes made her lower her eyes, while a quick, defensive pink flooded her cheeks. "I—I suppose I am a bit funny and gauche and therefore a good form of amusement," she muttered.

"Good lord!" Abruptly Burke was leaning across the table. "Good lord, child, I didn't bring you here to laugh at you. What an idea!"

"Why—did you bring me, then?"

"When we've eaten I'll tell you," he said.

But she was suddenly possessed by the rebellion he had questioned. So she was alone in the world and inclined to be shy—of men. But that, she thought hotly, didn't turn her into a complete fool. She wasn't fooled into thinking that this rich stranger saw anything very attractive in Laura Damien's typist. "I want to know now," she said, her chin lifting.

"Do you?" His eyes amusedly travelled her flushed young face. "Still suspicious of me, Rea Glyn?"

"Why shouldn't I be? I hardly know you—Mr. Ryeland."

"Hasn't the boa-constrictor enlightened you as to my family background?" He laughed softly, turning from her as the wine-waiter came to the table. He studied the list and finally ordered a bottle of Montrachet. Then he sat in a small inscrutable silence until the waiter brought the Montrachet, but once it was poured and Rea was holding her glass, with its delicate, cool stem, he said:

"Drink up and be merry, Rea, for in just five minutes I'm going to propose to you."

Rea just stared, and all the colour fled from her face as she absorbed the utter incredibility of his remark. The man was mad! Mentally deranged by that mysterious sojourn of his in Peru. Why, oh, why had she come here with him? She should have gone back to the hotel, to dine in the noisy but comparatively sane company of Laura Damien. . . .

"No, I'm not out of my mind, Rea," Burke said, the sparkle of the wine he was sipping reflected in his eyes.

"You must be!" Rea retorted. "Asking—asking someone you hardly know to—to marry you!"

"Asking someone I think I could trust and depend on to marry me," he amended.

"But—why?" Rea was caught in bewilderment and shock like a small fly in a web, her eyes imploring a sane explanation of him. "This is crazy—crazy!"

"Not so, my dear." Burke shook his head. "I've a perfectly sane and straightforward reason for wanting a wife, believe me. We'll discuss our nuptials after the feast, shall we?"

With the arrival of coffee, Burke was ready to present Rea with an explanation for his curious proposal. He leant his elbows on the table, watching her with eyes that had gone so serious he suddenly seemed older, even rather tired. "As I said, Rea, I didn't bring you here to make fun of you. You do believe that, don't you?"

"I—I don't know what I believe, to tell you the truth," Rea replied. "This is quite the most fantastic thing I've ever had happen to me."

"I can well believe that," he agreed. "On the face of it, a proposal of marriage from a stranger is fantastic. But I'm hoping that after I've explained the situation to you, you won't feel it so fantastic after all." Then he sat back, searching his breast pocket for a cigarette-case. "Do you smoke?" he queried. Rea shook her head, and he lit a cigarette for himself, shaking out the match with a rather impatient hand. Rea realized, with something of amazement, that he was almost as nervous as she was.

He took two or three hard puffs at the cigarette, his eyes narrowing against the smoke as it wreathed up about his dark face. Then he said abruptly: "I've a grandfather, Rea, who is a throwback. He belongs to a past era; the sort of era when family pride and a selfless devotion to the demands of that pride were held above all things. It isn't snobbery, exactly, but it's something ineradicable. He feels that to be born a Ryeland carries with it certain obligations—obligations which I do not feel disposed to meet. In short, Rea, I'm expected to marry for the sole purpose of producing the next Ryeland. My grandfather, who is eighty-five and in precarious health, has presented me with a problem I highly resent, yet which, for sentimental reasons, I must appear to bring to fruition for him."

Burke carefully flicked ash into the ashtray, his eyes steady on Rea's small, intent face. "I had a younger brother, Philip, whom my grandfather worshipped. All his hopes and joys were centred in and around Phil—but just over a year ago, while Phil was helping with the harvesting on one of the estate farms, he was killed by a threshing machine. The shock nearly killed my grandfather. But following on top of that came something else, something that would have broken him completely if he had come to learn of it. As boys, both Phil and I used to be pals with a girl from one of the local farms, a girl called Dani. She was a lovely, quicksilver kind of kid, whose parents were ambitious for her.

"Right from a tot they'd had her taught dancing, and when she was sixteen she left the farm to go and live in London with an aunt, so that she might attend a London school of ballet. She was quick and lovely and talented; with the passing of the years she achieved her parents' ambition and became a successful dancer. I, in the meantime, was travelling the globe. Phil was busy farming, and loving every moment of it. Then, like a bolt out of the blue, finding me in the heart of Peru, came the news that poor old Phil had been killed."

Burke's gaze dropped away from Rea's face; he moodily contemplated the smouldering tip of his cigarette. "I came back to England, naturally. I came back to a very sick old man, and a letter from Dani's aunt, now living here in Hastings. That letter contained a second shock for me—Dani was dead. She had died giving birth to my brother Phil's child; only the aunt was aware that the two had been lovers. Dani's parents, she wrote, were not prepared to take the child. And she had plans of her own which did not include him; she wanted to go and live in Canada with her sister. In short, she wanted to know whether I'd be prepared to accept the responsibility of the child—if not, she thought he should be put in an orphanage."

Burke's brows drew harshly together above the sapphire eyes. "I was appalled by such an idea. The boy was my nephew, Phil's child—a Ryeland!" Now Burke shrugged, a small, unamused smile twisting his well shaped mouth.

"The child has been in my care ever since." His smile deepened, losing some of its bitterness. "With this child ready made on my hands, Rea, half my grandfather's whim is met. But to give the plot reality, I must produce a mother for the boy. So I'm asking you, in all seriousness, to consider the job. I promise you it will be a much more congenial one than the one you have at present. You'll have no messy typewriters to contend with, nor the Damien braying in your ears day and night. I live in the heart of Somerset, among apple orchards and fields of wheat as high as your throat. And all I ask of you is that you marry me—in name only."

Rea drew a deep, gasping breath, staring at this incredible stranger, who presented her with such an incredible proposal. He had promised an end to fantasy, but she felt more than ever that she was living a fantasy.

"I—I don't think I could agree to—to deceive an old man," she murmured.

"Not even an old man who isn't in the best of health and who would be highly delighted to have a great-grandson—his very own, remember—placed in his arms before he dies?"

"It—it still wouldn't be right." Rea's eyes were large in her pale face; her small, thin hands were locked together on the edge of the table. "Supposing he found out? Think what it would do to him! You say he has pride. Why, he would feel that you had deliberately set out to injure his pride."

"I don't think he's very likely to find out, Rea. We're quite cut off from civilisation at King's Beeches, you know. Even so, who's to dispute my word if I say this child is mine?" He stared straight into Rea's eyes, and she flinched a little from the sudden flashing arrogance in his eyes. "It might interest you to know that as far as I'm concerned Peter is mine. He's mine in that the girl who gave birth to him meant—meant rather a lot to me." Burke ground out his cigarette with hard, angry movements of his hand. "On that count will you accept my proposal? Where's the harm? You'll be making an old, tired man very happy, and you'll be giving a grand little youngster someone he can call mother."

But Rea was floundering, bewildered, panicky. She was like someone who has swum out into unknown waters; she knew a desperate desire to turn back and find solidity and sanity again, but Burke held her in the deeps, dominated her with his blue eyes. "I—I don't know what to say to you," she whispered. "I don't know how to answer you."

"Look," abruptly he leant across the table and pressed her cold, clenched hands, "let's suspend discussion of all this until you've seen Peter. Let him be the deciding factor. Tomorrow I'll take you to see him. He still lives, for the present, with that aunt of Dani's." Then he turned in his chair to beckon the waiter. He settled the bill and he and Rea made their way out of the restaurant. It had grown colder and Rea shivered as they stepped into the street. "Will you come tomorrow?" Burke asked as he handed her into the car.

She hesitated, staring up into his dark face. He was a stranger—she knew nothing of him beyond the things Laura Damien had told her, and those things did not make for very much confidence in him. Hard, arrogant, without affection!

And she—she was a stranger to him.

Her hand found and clutched his sleeve. "Why do you ask this of me? All you know of me is that I work for Laura Damien."

"On the contrary, I know that you're nineteen years old, quite alone in the world, and gifted with patience. Patience is a sign of virtue, isn't it?" The words came smilingly. "Oh, you're what I want right enough, Rea Glyn. Now, will you come and see Peter tomorrow?"

And as though the words came of their own volition, she heard herself say: "All right, Mr. Ryeland, I'll come."

CHAPTER THREE

WHILE Rea and Laura Damien sat at breakfast, Laura suddenly glanced up from the Sunday newspaper to demand: "What do you intend doing with your self today?"

"If it's all right with you, Mrs. Damien, I'll do a little exploring this afternoon," Rea said.

Laura looked inquisitive. "With some seashore Lothario?" she queried, and one of her painted brows shot high as Rea uncontrollably blushed. "I see," she drawled, "so you did go gallivanting last night. Well, don't get too involved with this young man; I've decided to go back to London tomorrow."

Rea's startled gasp was revealing—both to herself and to the scornfully amused Laura. She had so little time to decide now—so little time! If she said yes to Burke Ryeland's amazing proposal an entirely new life would open for her; a life devoid of hothouse hotels and a wearisome round of hours spent pounding a typewriter and catering to the whims of this brassy, self-indulgent, self-satisfied woman. If she said no, the tentacles of the painted Laura would stay wrapped around her, for years—for ever!

Burke Ryeland had said he would pick her up at two o'clock, and dead on two Rea was waiting, wrapped in the smooth camel-hair coat that had been her father's last present to her.

Burke sounded the motor-horn and Rea swung round from the window, smiling shyly when she saw him. He leant across to open the door of the car for her, and she slipped in beside him, aware that her heart was beating very fast all of a sudden. "So you came?" Burke murmured, swinging the car out from the kerb.

"Didn't you think I would, Mr. Ryeland?" she asked.

"I didn't really know what to think—Miss Glyn." He grinned at her. "Do you think you could bring yourself to call me Burke—I think we might safely say we've reached the Christian name stage?"

"All right." She sat slim and straight against the scarlet leather of the car, her hands folded primly in her lap, her fair fringe dancing as the car picked up speed and the whip of the wind came at them.

"Did the boa-constrictor want to know where you were going?" Burke enquired.

Rea grinned. "She's got it into her head that I'm playing fast and loose with a poor fisher-lad. I've been warned not to get too involved. She—we're going back to London tomorrow."

Burke shot a quick, questioning glance at Rea. "You're going, are you?"

Rea glanced down rather confusedly at her folded hands. "I—I don't know."

"Do you want to go?" Burke insisted.

She didn't answer, and now his glance of interrogation held a slight impatience—an impatience that dwindled, however, as he took note of the worried, indecisive way she chewed her lips with small, childish teeth. "Don't do that," he said, "you'll make your lip bleed."

"W-what?" Her eyes came to his face and he saw that they were wearing again that look they had worn last night, that startled-doe look, as though she prepared for precipitate flight from the slavering jaws of a rather middle-aged lion. He smiled sardonically. "Did you lie awake all last night, tossing and turning and still wondering whether you'd eaten dinner with a madman?" he queried.

"H-how did you guess?" She attempted to speak lightly, but was defeated both by agitation and a deep blush. For she had lain awake, going restlessly over and over his story in her mind, knowing it to be a sincere one, yet knowing, too, that she shrank from the many lies that would be involved if she agreed to become part of his plot to deceive his grandfather.

"I knew, naturally, that you were worried," he replied. "But you need only regard the whole thing as a job, you know." His glance travelled up and down the flushed curve of her profile. "I shall provide you with a weekly or a monthly income, as you wish, making you independent in that respect," and as he saw her bite her lip again, added: "If we regard the whole thing on business lines, you will, I think, be less embarrassed by the necessary marriage ceremony. And that reminds me, I forgot to ask you last night whether you had any romantic entanglements. Have you?"

She shook her head quickly.

She heard him laugh. "That would have been awkward, some fiery young Romeo demanding my release of his Juliet. Tell me, Rea, do you like children?"

"I've not had much to do with them," she admitted. "I think I like them."

"You'll like Peter. He's a grand little chap."

"How old is he?"

"Five months." Burke's lips quirked on a knowing smile. "Are you wondering how I'm going to explain my possession of a five-month-old son to my grandfather?"

She nodded.

"Well, I shall prevaricate, naturally. If you agree to marry me, and we get married, I shall lie about the date of our marriage. It's in a good cause."

Rea bit her lip. "Do you have to do that? Couldn't you tell the truth?"

"My grandfather wouldn't accept Peter if he knew the truth. That darn pride we spoke about." The words came flatly, crisply.

Rea frowned perplexedly. "You said—you said he worshipped your brother."

"Worshipped him for a model of virtue." Burke's shrug was full of cynicism. "It wouldn't do for that stern old man to learn that Phil could be—well, as foolish as the rest of us. So I shall lie, quite flagrantly, and young Peter shall come into his own." He swung the car into a quiet side road with these words, and in a moment it had come to a standstill.

The house was neat and small, with pink curtains at the windows, a cream-painted gate and a rather threadbare square of front lawn. Rea followed Burke along the crazy-paving path to the front door, standing quiet beside him as he plied the knocker. This time yesterday she was caught up in a wild, fantastic plot, half promised to this man, who was ready to deceive his own flesh and blood so that the son of a dancing girl might become the heir of ancient, beautiful King's Beeches.

Then the door of the little house came open and a very thin, dark little woman, with inquisitive, boot-button eyes, came out upon the step. She grasped Burke's arms and laughed up into his face. "Hullo, love!" she exclaimed, then she glanced at Rea and her laughter gave way to open surprise.

"This is Rea Glyn, Polly," Burke said, releasing himself from the woman's hands and pulling Rea to his side. "I think I'm going to marry her, Polly."

"Are you, now?" The little woman stepped back into the tiny hall of the house, beckoning them to follow her. When they stepped into the kitchen, she swung round and frankly examined Rea with her darting brown eyes. "So you think you're getting married?" she said to Burke. "Aren't you sure?"

He laughed and Rea felt his hard fingers close about her wrist. "She wants to ask Peter's permission. Go and get him, Polly."

"So she knows she'll have a ready-made baby on her hands."

"Peter's the main attraction, on the level."

Polly Wilmot gave Rea a long stare. "Most girls would put King's Beeches first. Don't you?" she asked, a trifle rudely.

Rea coloured warmly. "I've never been there," she replied.

"Never—" the woman's eyes went narrow as she turned them upon Burke. "Isn't this the one your grandfather wants you to marry?" she demanded.

"No, Polly." He spoke crisply, with a sudden touch of impatience, it seemed to Rea. "Now hop along and get young Peter. I want Rea to see him."

"I'll put the kettle on for some tea first." The brisk, inquisitive Polly went out to the scullery to do so. When she came back into the kitchen, she said to Rea: "Take a chair, young lady." Then she departed for the upper regions of the little house.

Burke laughed, watching Rea as she nervously took a chair. "Polly's bark is worse than her bite, Rea," he said. "I knew her very well—oh, some years ago. Which doesn't alter the fact, however, that I shan't be sorry when she's safely tucked away in Canada. Our little deception should be fairly foolproof, then . . . Ah, here she is with the boy!" He stepped forward to take the baby from Polly as she came in with him.

"Go easy, lad," she said, "he's asleep."

"Does a mighty lot of sleeping, doesn't he, Polly?" Burke held the baby with a serious masculine care and peered down into the small, sleep-flushed face.

"I daresay you did the same, at his age." Polly shot Rea a quizzical look. "Men!" she grunted.

Rea half-smiled as Burke came to her side and carefully placed the baby in her lap, pulling back the blue shawl so that she might get a better look at him. Black, black hair curled in tiny, endearing ringlets along his forehead, and his plump fists were doubled against plump, rosy cheeks. "Why, he's perfectly beautiful!" Rea gasped, an enchanted child herself as she gazed at the child in her lap.

"He's grand!" Burke said, and there was such a throb of sudden feeling in his voice that Rea knew, instinctively, that he was visualizing the child's mother. How had Laura Damlen described her—wild as a hawk and lovely as a firefly? Rea bent her glance more closely over the sleeping baby, feeling rather embarrassed, as though she had had a stolen glimpse into Burke Ryeland's heart.

"I'm going to make that tea," Polly Wilmot said, and marched off to do so. But at the door, she turned and studied Burke. "When are you two getting married?" she demanded.

He lounged against the mantelpiece beside Rea, hands in the pockets of his tweed jacket. "If Rea's agreeable," he said, "I rather fancy this coming Friday."

Rea glanced up, her eyes wide on his face, her cheeks flooding with a sudden violent pink. "So—so soon?" she gasped.

He laughed and lifted his black brows at Polly. "My bride-to-be doesn't sound wildly enthusiastic, does she? Do you suppose she's feeling jittery?"

Polly snorted, her sharp eye moving to Rea. "All brides-to-be are jittery—it's part of their attraction." With which broadside she disappeared into the scullery, from whence came the brisk chink of china and the blatant whistling of the kettle.

"Well, Rea?" Burke said, "will you consent to be my lawfully wedded on Friday?" He watched her, his blue quizzical eyes travelling her rather frightened face. "My dear girl, why are you looking like that?" he exclaimed. "I should think you'd be excited, rather than otherwise, at the prospect of getting away from Laura Damien's mad noise. Don't you consider me an improvement on the boa-constrictor?" He held her gaze, his smile assuming an indulgent quality. "Do say yes, Rea. I shall be most cut if you don't, you know."

But Rea didn't return his smile. She bent over the baby, so warm and rosy and unconscious of being the centre of a drama Burke Ryeland chose to treat with lightness. "Don't you think—don't you think you ought to marry someone you're more sure of?" she murmured. "I'm such a complete stranger to you—a—a person who knows nothing of your way of life. I'm totally inadequate—can't you see that?"

"I'm perfectly content with what I see," he responded lazily. "I know I don't have to hold you up to the light to see whether you're full of hidden vices. And it occurs to me that if you've borne patiently with the demands of Laura Damien for nine long months, then you're far from inadequate."

"But—marriage—" Rea shivered slightly. "I'd be perfectly willing to be Peter's nursemaid—"

"You have to marry me." The words came crisply. "You have to become Peter's mother and my wife. The situation isn't at all complicated." She heard him laugh. "It's a perfectly beautiful one. You acquire leisure to enjoy life, while I acquire my grandsire's pat on the head for developing into a good, dutiful lad at long last." Then his tone abruptly altered, lost laughter and grew decisive. "Make up your mind, Rea, you come with me, or you go with Laura Damien. I can give you freedom, though you become my wife. She'll tie you to that damned busy typewriter of hers for the next twenty years. Some prospect, eh?"

Abruptly he bent over the baby Rea held so carefully. He touched the damp, dark hair with a gentle finger. "You said you thought him beautiful—and he is. I want to take him to King's Beeches, where he belongs. Help me to take him, Rea."

And then, as Burke caressed the baby's head, he awoke with a tiny gurgle, waved his plump fists and stretched in Rea's arms. And Rea's heart jumped into her throat, for the eyes that shot wide open, staring up at her, were as blue, and as darkly fringed, as the eyes of Burke Ryeland—this man who asked her to become the wife he would never kiss.

"Next—Friday, did you say?" She spoke almost upon a whisper.

Burke grew very still, his caressing finger pausing upon the baby's head. Slowly he turned his head and met Rea's confused, still rather panicky eyes. He searched them deeply, and when they didn't waver from his, he nodded.

As they drove back to the hotel, Burke said: "What are you going to tell Laura?"

"What do you want me to tell her?" Rea countered.

He smiled slightly. "Will you mind saying that you're merely taking on a new job? I think the less that rather loud-mouthed party knows about our plans, the better."

Rea studied his profile with something of curiosity. "Why do you dislike her so much—Burke?" she asked, and she flushed, speaking his name. Though she had now committed herself to his amazing, frightening marriage plan, she still felt awkward in his presence, gauche and young and full of shyness. He was so sure of himself, so at ease all the time. Travelled and learned and worldly—and rather cynical, in the way of such people, despite his determination to take his brother's baby home to King's Beeches with the minimum of hurt and disillusionment to his grandfather. Despite that hurt he carried, deep within himself; that untouchable, very personal hurt which mention of the girl Dani could bring to his eyes, darkening their vivid blue.

"I don't dislike Laura Damien," he drawled. "I can't work up that much feeling about her. She merely desecrates the landscape for me. As a country boy, born and bred, I appreciate beauty and pleasant solitude, and Madame Damien possesses neither. She's a predatory mammoth, ever hungry and ever on the hunt."

Rea's laughter held a half-ashamed note. "Oh, you exaggerate!" she protested. "She's rather loud, I know, but she isn't entirely unlikeable. One has to admire her energy. And she writes well; you've got to admit that."

He shrugged. "I'm not addicted myself to her kind of desert rapturizing, but I suppose she has a certain flair for making young female hearts beat a little faster." He shot an amused, speculative side-glance at Rea. "Are you addicted to desert rapture, Rea? Do you have romantic moon-drenched dreams?"

She smiled and shook her head. "I'm not the romantic type," she murmured.

"Aren't you, Rea?" He was still smiling. "Perhaps that's just as well considering you're upon the threshold of making a quite unromantic marriage. Tell me, now that you've seen young Peter you've quite shed all your misgivings, haven't you?"

"I—I like him enormously." She twisted her hands together in her lap. Talk of this—this marriage still brought her heart into her throat; still sent a wild dart of panic shooting through her. There would be lies, fabrications, and she shrank from them. There would be an old, proud, startled man to deal with—from where, out of her small store of self-confidence, would she find the equanimity to face him? What if he saw through Burke's deception? What if he scorned her as a wife for Burke?

"Still worrying about how my grandfather will react to my sudden production of a wife and child?" Burke queried.

She nodded. "What will you say? How will you explain us?"

"The situation will explain itself, I think, Rea."

"Explain—but how?" Rea cast a startled side-glance at his calm, sardonic profile.

"Well, the fact of the matter is," Burke drawled, "he's already half inclined to suspect that I've been conducting a liaison of some sort, owing to my frequent weekend absences from home—my visits to little Peter, in short. Therefore all I need to do at this stage is play the repentant but hopeful rake." Burke smiled rakishly. "The old boy has always had a tendency to regard me as such—a girl in every equatorial outpost, you know—so you can rest assured he'll not probe too deeply into any sudden marriage of mine. As far as he's concerned, Rea, I joined the ranks of the damned and the Bohemian years ago, when I published my first book. I was a Ryeland, you see!" Burke pulled a wry mouth and swung the grey car round a corner, straight into a high breath of wind with sudden fine rain in it. "I was a Ryeland, and though it was perfectly all right for me to pitch hay and sow turnips and help the cows have their offspring—when I wasn't looking eligible at county meets and balls—it wasn't all right for me to dabble my fingers in literary ink and my toes in Nile water. Therefore, since the day I insisted upon doing both, leaving the entire running of the Ryeland holdings to my brother, every one of my actions has been automatically suspect in my grandfather's eyes."

Sympathy was in Rea's quick glance at his profile, upon which cynicism was stamped hard in this moment. "Now you've had to give up your travelling and your writing, haven't you?" she murmured.

He shrugged. "Phil loved the cows and the turnips; the estate and Somerset. I love Somerset—with time the rest will come, I hope! One thing is certain, I couldn't have borne giving myself entirely to the demands of King's Beeches, hence this marriage idea. My grandfather gets what he's always wanted—Phil's son; and I shall cease to be regarded in the county as a likely candidate for the marriage stakes." He shot a grin at

Rea. "And you, my child, acquire freedom from drudgery, therefore the few necessary lies we shall be obliged to tell will be well worth the telling, in my opinion."

That evening, just before dinner, Rea told Laura that she wouldn't be going back to London with her the following morning. Laura looked staggered, and then a heavy frown came down over her face like a storm cloud. "I'll be damned if you'll walk out on me like this!" she thundered. "A little chit like you! You'll go when I say so."

Rea drew back from this display of nasty temper; though partly expected it still had the power to set her nerves jumping. "I'm sorry, Mrs. Damien," she said, "but I've been offered another job, one that—that suits me better. I'm sorry to give you such short notice, but it can't be helped."

Laura's lowering stare was thick with suspicion. "Who the hell have you met?" she demanded. "Who has offered you another job?"

But Rea stood dumb before her, her face pale, her eyes wide with a frightened but quite determined defiance.

Laura stepped to her and gripped her shoulders, giving her a shake. "You underhanded little snip;" she growled. "You've been playing about with some man, haven't you?"

Rea shook her head, rather wildly. "No! That isn't true! I'm—I'm tired of typing work, that's all. I want a change. I'm going into the country to look after a little boy."

Laura's wide, lush mouth expressed a frank and scornful disbelief. "There's a big boy involved here, I can tell by the way of you."

"You're—you're insulting!" Rea gasped. The nerves that were drumming hard under her skin and in her throat were making her feel a little sick—she wanted to run from this room, from Laura's horrible insinuations. "I've told you the truth," she cried, "I'm going into the country to look after a little boy. You've no right to think—what you're thinking."

"Is that so?" Laura slowly turned from the dressing-table and leant against it, her eyes travelling up and down the slight figure of Rea. She looked heavily malicious. "I'll tell you what right I've got. I could hold you to a weeks' notice."

"Why, I've not been paid any wages for three weeks, Mrs. Damien," Rea flashed back. "You can't force me to abide by a contract you've already broken."

Laura stared, and then, quite unexpectedly, she broke into a husky hoot of laughter. "Hell's bells, whoever the guy is, he's woken you up with a vengeance. I'll say that for him." With a rustle of cerise silk she moved to the bed, where her handbag lay. She took it up, opened it and drew six five-pound notes from her wallet. She brought them to Rea, took hold of her hand and laid them in her palm, closing her fingers over them. She was smiling in her old complacent way. "Take a tip from me, honey, have your bit of fun, but don't cry when the morning comes—and it always comes."

Rea stared at the money in her hand. "What you're thinking is—is quite wrong," she muttered.

"Is it?" Laura laughed again. "Look, sweetie, you can't fool me! I'm Laura Damien, remember! I've been around! I know you're mixed up with a man, you've got all the symptoms. So what? I'm broadminded enough to think it about time, to tell you the truth, even though you're leaving me in a bit of a hole."

Abruptly she reached out a large hand; took hold of Rea's chin and jerked her head up. She searched Rea's confused and guilty eyes. "You've worked damn quick, haven't you, honey? I shouldn't have thought there were many Romeos for you to get involved with in this one-horse town." A malicious grin split open her large, painted mouth. "You little slyboots, you! With all that big-eyed syrup about not being interested in men!" She gave Rea's chin a mocking brush with her fist. "Well, have fun, honey; eat your cake, but as I've already advised, don't cry when you wake up one morning and find that all you've got left is the cake-stand. Cake, my little innocent, has a way of packing its bag and vanishing with the dawn. All the same," her mouth held a sudden lush curve, "I will say that cake is nice while it lasts. I hope he's nice and plummy—plain cake can go stale. Is he plummy?"

Rea wouldn't answer, but somewhere below the guilt and the resentful embarrassment she couldn't help feeling, a small flare of amusement shot up. Burke Ryeland, she thought, could certainly be called plum cake—with icing!

CHAPTER FOUR

BURKE'S grey car swung in between tall, elegant iron gates and he called out a greeting to the little man in breeches and gaiters who had come out from a stone house by the gates to unlock them.

" 'Tis a grand evenin', maister," the man replied, wiping grubby hands up and down the sides of his breeches, his eyes upon Rea as he spoke.

"Fine evening, Simon," Burke called back, laughing as the car turned a bend in the drive and they lost the little man and his staring, wondering eyes. "Our first encounter with curiosity, Rea," Burke murmured.

Rea's heart was thumping wildly, and when little Peter stirred in her arms, wriggling in his shawl, she drew him closer to her, finding a small measure of reassurance and comfort in the plump, warm weight of him. He was exceedingly lovable; a laughing, contented baby, who already seemed to sense that though new arms held him, they were arms that welcomed him.

The thought moved warm in her and some of the nervous tension she had been feeling all day began to steal out of her. Now, after all, there was no going back. Now she was Burke's wife and well and truly joined with him in his game of deception—yet it wasn't a deception to despise, she kept on telling herself that! He only wanted to give love and security to little Peter and he wasn't cheating his grandfather in any way. Peter was entirely the Ryeland the old man so longed for; the key of the future; the small vessel who would ensure the continuation of the Ryeland line. . . .

Then Burke murmured beside her: "We're home, Rea."

She glanced up—and gave a breathless gasp of pure delight. King's Beeches lay before her, its Tudor beauty serenely dreaming in an orange glow of fading sunset.

The house had a grace that took Rea's breath; a beauty of line and structure that was like the fine, indestructible bones under a truly beautiful face. It rose naturally out of the smooth, velvety turf of its lawns, stood warm and ancient and tawny against a perfect framework of autumn evening sky and rolling Mendip hills.

The car drew in against wide stone steps to the front door and Burke turned to smile at Rea. "Well," he asked, "all prepared to be possessed by this ancient mass of mere bricks and mortar?"

"Oh, don't! Don't speak like that! King's Beeches is superb!" Her eyes came rather dazedly to his face. "Surely you must love it? How can you not love it?"

"I see a beautiful, indestructible building, Rea, but I refuse to let it possess me—in the way it has always possessed my grandfather. In the way it possessed my brother." Then his smile softened as he studied the way Rea had little Peter cuddled against her, the very picture of young, serious motherhood. "I must say," he said, leaning forward to peer down at the cooing and completely contented baby, "that you and young Peter have lost very little time falling deeply in love."

"Well, we've so much in common," she smiled. "We're both grateful orphans, sheltering under your wing." And as she spoke the wide stretch of Burke's shoulders above her and Peter seemed to lend a veritable truth to her words. Though this strange marriage she had made was one of mere convenience, still it was a marriage, and she bore Burke's name, held the right to stand at his side, and call him husband. She felt her heart jump in her side like a startled bird at the thought. This distinguished and accomplished stranger was her husband—her husband!

Then the great iron-bound door of the house came open and Burke called out to the stout, immaculately clad figure who stood in the arched aperture: "I've some surprising news, Tolliver; I've brought home a wife."

"Indeed, sir?" The butler came down the wide stone steps to the car and politely accepted the suitcases Burke handed out to him, murmuring a deferential welcome to Rea, no hint of surprise denting his sauve impassivity.

"How's my grandfather?" Burke enquired, climbing from the car and taking the baby from Rea, who nervously swung her slim legs to the ground and followed him up the steps to the house.

"Your grandfather is quite well, sir. His rheumatism has hardly troubled him these past two weeks. Possibly owing to the fine spell of weather we've been having." The butler stood to one side to allow Rea to precede him into the hall, and as she did so, she met the fleeting glance he cast at her and then at the baby in Burke's arms. An hysterical desire to laugh suddenly spiralled through her. Poor man, having to look polite and unsurprised when he was very likely wanting to drop his lip and say, "Oh!"

The hall was immense, with big bronze wall-sconces throwing golden light along the oak-panelled walls, and a pyramid of sweet-smelling pear logs glowing and leaping in the wide mouth of a big stone fireplace. Light was lost overhead, however, in a vaulted mass of heavy black beams, but right at the end of the hall Rea could see the carved balusters of a handsome double staircase.

Rea knew a sense of stepping back into time. A door seemed to close on all she had known of the busy, hurrying modern world and another seemed to open, showing her how a house belonging to a past era, and a way of life belonging to that same era, could continue quietly down the years like an unbroken, powerful thread, never snapped through the long, long years.

Then she jumped, hearing the butler say: "Mr. Philip is in the library, Mr. Burke."

"Come along, Rea," Burke said, and she crossed the hall with him. She was quite cold, though the hall was warm, and her legs felt strange and rubbery, moving automaton-like beside the long legs of Burke. She childishly, nervously brushed at the fringe as Burke paused before a door, rapped a tattoo upon it with his knuckles and then swung it open in a lordly fashion, holding Peter in one arm and propelling Rea into the room with the other.

The only light in the room shone from a reading-lamp, for the fire had burned down to a steady red glow. Pipe smoke lay thick over the room, dancing blue round the bowl of the reading-lamp, round the white head of the man who sat reading before the fire.

He glanced up slowly, taking his pipe from his mouth. His eyes, Rea thought, must once have been as blue as Burke's, but now their blue was dimmed by great age, The fine bones of his face stood out sharply, the hawk nose giving him an arrogant, unfriendly look. He stared hard at Rea, and she gulped under that stare, pressing back for reassurance against the solid warmth of Burke's arm.

"So you've come home!" the old man grunted at last, his glance moving with abrupt sharpness to the shawl-enveloped bundle in Burke's arm. The sounds issuing from that bundle were unmistakably the cooings and chuckles of a baby talking to itself, and the pale, hard eyes watched, startled, the small gloved fist waving about in the air above the shawl.

"I've brought you home a great-grandson," Burke said quietly. "Is it—all right?"

A strange quality of stillness lay over that silver-haired, proud and upright figure then. His stillness, in fact, spread right round the room, gripped both Rea and Burke, and all that was left was the faint splutter of the low-burning fire and the chirrupings of little Peter.

Then the old man stirred, drew a deep breath. "You have your nerve, my boy, marching in here and proudly displaying your brat. And who's this?" He threw out a hand towards Rea.

"My wife, sir." Burke smiled as he spoke—a curious smile, Rea noted, as she glanced up at him. It held an imperious quality, making his decisive nostrils flare slightly, as though he verged upon a display of anger.

"Your wife, eh?" The pale blue eyes raked the slender figure so tense beside Burke, hazel eyes enormous in a pale, triangular face, straight child's hair cut to small ears with a pixie slant to them. She looked startlingly young and frail against the dark bulk of Burke. Barely a wife! Barely a mother!

"Ye gods, Burke," the old man exploded, "what have you been up to?"

"Obeying your instructions, my dear grandsire—getting myself married—getting myself a son." Now he carried the baby across the room and without further ado lowered him into the old man's arms. "Say you're pleased," Burke murmured, a slightly rakish grin coming to his face. "I've done my duty by you now, sir."

The thick white eyebrows of old Philip Ryeland shot rapidly up and down. He sat stiffly, half scared, it seemed, of the wriggling bundle so suddenly in his arms. "A boy, is it, eh?" He carefully prodded Peter's cheek, as though to assure himself that the baby was real. Then he shot a disgruntled glare at Burke. "Dash it all, Burke, why can't you do things in a regular manner? You're too dashed cosmopolitan, that's your trouble. Too much like that flighty little French fool your father saw fit to marry!"

"What if I am, sir?" Burke's eyes met and held the old man's. "I've not done a bad job with this laddie, have I?" His tone was half jocular, half proud, and Rea was full of wonder at the ease with which he had convinced his grandfather that the child was his. She watched the tableau before her with large eyes, the collected group that represented three generations of the Ryeland line. She felt very much an intruder in that moment. The old man had looked at her with such scornful eyes; no wifc for a Ryeland, those eyes had said. No fit mate for the big, dark Burke Ryeland, who could have had any woman he cast those flame-blue eyes over. She shivered and drew back into the shadows by the door, wanting to run from those faded blue eyes that scorned her, that looked for the maturity of a real wife and mother in her—and found it not.

The arrival of a child in the house created quite a stir. Two of the maids were hurriedly despatched upstairs to prepare a room for Rea and Peter, while out in the kitchen the elderly cook, under Burke's authoritative direction, sterilized the baby's bottle and carefully tested the temperature of the milk. Then Burke carried the bottle to the library, where Rea was installed upon a big couch in front of the fire, soothing the baby, who was now demanding his supper, Burke handed the bottle to Rea. "You know how, I suppose?" he murmured, leaning over the back of the couch and watching the tentative way she approached the bottle to the baby's mouth. "Let him gobble a little of it, then let him take a breather. Do it in stages."

Rea nodded, and he straightened up as his grandfather came into the room, announcing that dinner was being held back until the baby had been fed. Then Moira, one of the maids—a sensible young thing—would put him to bed for Rea.

"You're being awfully decent about all this, sir," Burke said, watching his grandfather approach the fireplace and stand before it, his eyes upon Rea and the child.

"Did you think I wouldn't be?" the old man shot a sharp glance at Burke, his white brows merging in a quick frown. "Got yourself involved with a chit and thought I'd be annoyed, eh?"

Burke was looking quizzical as he played his game of repentant rake, one eye, at the same time, marking the flush that lit Rea's cheek. "I'd be grateful if you'd extend your kindness to Rea, sir." He smiled slightly. "After all, she isn't only my wife, she's Peter's mother."

The old man's glance went again to Rea. His frown was very heavy. Without her coat she was thinner than ever. She looked as though she'd blow away in the first strong wind that came down from the Mendips! No, he couldn't pretend he was pleased with this pale chit, but the boy was fine, a real Ryeland—and devilishly like young Philip. He drew a harsh sigh.

Philip Ryeland stared hard at Rea—and Rea shivered under that stare. She knew what he was thinking; it was almost as though his mind had opened in that moment to let her read what was written there. He was plainly rejecting her appeal to Burke in any physical sense, but that rejection, she saw, was brought up sharp against the indisputable evidence of Peter in her arms. Beautiful, plump, very real Peter, his blue eyes fixed upon her face as he sucked himself drowsy with milk, his dark, warm head cradled against the slight curve of her breast.

Then she stiffened, a curious little tremor wending its way through her, for Burke had leant over the back of the couch and lightly tweaked her hair. She glanced up at him and tentatively returned his smile. "You look tired, my dear," he murmured.

"Oh, I'm all right." She was confused by his concern for her.

"I think you'd better get to bed as soon as you've had your dinner," he said.

Rea's bedroom was huge. The light of two oil-lamps didn't penetrate the whole of it and the flare of the log fire threw long, goblin shadows up the walls, whose paper bore great bunches of cabbage-roses, looking more like lopped heads in the dancing light.

Peter's cradle, which Burke had brought down with them in the car, stood beside Rea's bed, a big four-poster, complete with a draped tester. The posts of the bed were ornately carved, the dark wood matching the beams of the ceiling. Also heavily carved were the chairs, the chest of drawers and the enormous, cavernous wardrobe with its heavy double doors and silver handles.

Rea sat on the edge of her big bed and peered into Peter's cradle. He was soundly sleeping. This strange house didn't trouble him. He wasn't aware of the weird country noises beyond the casements; he didn't feel that at any moment the doors of that monster wardrobe would open and a mailed knight would step forth into this room—a ghostly descendant of this ancient house, who walked again its vast rooms and shadow-haunted galleries when night shut day from the sky and owls stared and hooted in the tall trees of the park. . . .

Rea shivered and told herself not to be a fool.

She rose from the bed and approached the nearest window, pulling aside the curtain and gazing out into the darkness. The draped ivy below the window rustled in the night air and the yelp of a prowling fox rose sharply above the stamping of horses from the stables.

There was no moon. The sky lay dark and impenetrable over the house and Rea felt very alone, very far from the busy, noisy world she had shared for nine months with Laura Damien.

She thought of her father—and of the little house they had lived in at Chingford; the little square house, with the little square garden her father had so loved to potter about in. So different from all this—the tall trees, the acres of smooth lawn, the intoxicating cider smell that stole through the partly open window. There had been just gentle, familiar routine; her father setting off in the morning for the Town Hall, where he worked in the Housing Department; she setting off for her classes at the secretarial college. . . .

But it had all collapsed, so suddenly, so finally—the long quiet evenings and the long quiet talks snatched out of her life; the world of love in her father's smile lost to her. Now all she had left was the memory of them.

Her breath caught on a sigh that was very close to a sob and she turned hurriedly from the window and set about preparing for bed. But the homesickness and the strangeness persisted like a spell. She turned out one of the lamps and lowered the other to a glimmer—telling herself she did this in case Peter should wake and need attention, but as she darted back to the big bed and climbed into it, her young, thin body was shrinking actively from the crowding shadows in the corners of the room.

She was drifting on the kindly edges of sleep when the door of her room opened.

It was a heavy door and it creaked slightly, the sound immediately arousing Rea. She lay against her mound of pillows, watching Burke's tall figure emerge out of the shadows. He came to the side of her bed and stood smiling down at her. "I came to see whether you were quite comfortable." His smile broadened. "Are you?"

"I feel rather lost," she murmured.

"You look it!" He walked round the bed and took a look at the soundly sleeping Peter. "Tomorrow we'll see about a nursery for this young man. Moira can have charge of him. She's good with children, I hear—has about eight or nine brothers and sisters."

"Oh, but that isn't necessary," Rea broke in quickly. "I don't mind looking after Peter. I—I'd like to look after him. It will give me something to do."

"Nonsense!" Burke laughed. "I didn't bring you here to turn you into a nursemaid—that would get Grandfather's goat! He has the rather old-fashioned idea that mothers spoil their sons."

"You—you feel that he really has accepted me as Peter's mother?" Rea spoke breathlessly, gathering a handful of the quilt in her agitation.

Burke fingered his chin a moment in a reflective manner, then he sat down on the bed, leaned forward and smilingly eased her fingers from their clutch upon the quilt. He took them into his large hand. "It's a little early yet to say exactly what he does think; he isn't an expansive person, as you may have noticed. He likes the boy, though—I probed that much out of him." Burke turned Rea's hand in his, his smile deepening at the smallness of it; it looked lost and rather helpless in the brown expanse of his palm. "I know all about you!" he said. "You're still worrying, aren't you?"

Her eyes wavered from his. "I—I can't help it. I don't think your grandfather likes me. I think I've come as a bit of a shock to him."

"Very probably." Burke's drawl held a deep amusement. "You have a singularly innocent look, my dear, and he doubtless feels, in the rather suspicious circumstances, that you're a case of hidden deeps under a deceptively quiet exterior. Do you mind so terribly—being thought a quiet jade?" Imperceptibly his fingers tightened on hers as he made this remark.

Rea's glance lifted tentatively to his face. It wore an amused indulgence, she saw; the same sort of indulgence he might show a perplexed child. "The point is," she said, "I actually feel a—a quiet jade." She grinned.

"Laura Damien would be amused. She thought me a priceless goody-goody."

"Did she accept, without question, your explanation of another job?" Burke asked, looking curious. He had meant to question Rea on this before, but the few days intervening before their marriage had been fairly busy ones and it had slipped his mind. It occurred to him now, however, that the brassy Laura had probably had quite a lot to say when Rea had handed in her notice; it wouldn't have suited Laura, losing the services of anyone as conscientious as this child.

Rea gave a breathless little laugh. "No, she didn't! She thought I had suddenly decided to count the world well lost for love. She wished me well and told me not to cry when—" Then Rea broke off, colouring as she remembered Laura's bawdy implications.

"Go on," Burke murmured.

But Rea shook her head. "It's nothing. She—she chose to think I intended doing something disreputable, that's all."

"I see." Burke, frowning, fingered the ring upon the small hand he held; the ring he had put there that morning.

There had been a little rain and then a little sunshine and the Registrar's office had been quiet and solemn and rather dusty and he had felt Rea actually shaking beside him as she had made her barely audible responses, her eyes over-large in her pale face. When he had put the wedding-ring on her finger she had looked ready to burst into tears. He had thought that she was suddenly afraid of him and he had said to her, as they drove to Polly Wilmot's to collect Peter: "Look, Rea, that marriage ceremony was only a necessary formality. You mustn't let the fact that I am now your husband worry you."

"It's just—I—I feel rather guilty," she had replied, and glancing quickly sideways at her he had realized that he had put the wrong interpretation upon her nervousness. She wasn't afraid of him as a man or a husband, he saw; she barely comprehended him as a husband, and as he watched her, she quickly pulled her glove on over the gleaming ring on her left hand

and he knew that she was attempting to thrust her feeling of guilt out of sight: attempting to forget that they intended turning the promises they had just made, one to the other, in that dusty, impersonal office, into a series of deliberate lies. To him the marriage was just a means to an end, that end being Peter's acceptance at King's Beeches without question and without suspicion. But he saw now that to Rea it was a dark step into the unknown, one she had not taken with ease, despite the release it afforded her from Laura Damien's exacting employment.

He remarked to her now, rather abruptly: "It's proof of your innate niceness, my child, that you've remained nice after nine months of that Damien woman's company." He released her hand and rose from the bed; stood very tall and broad beside it, glancing round the big, dim room. "Are you quite happy with this room, Rea?" he asked.

"Yes, thank you." She gave him a polite smile.

"I believe you think it a bit of a ballroom." A grin broke on his lips. "You'll get used to it. In about a week you'll be thoroughly at home here. You mustn't let my grandfather, or the servants, unnerve you. You won't, will you?"

"I'll try not to." Again her smile was the polite smile of a guest to her host. The gold ring glittering upon her finger meant nothing. She would never feel herself the mistress of this enormous and beautiful house; official wife to this tall, smiling, self-assured man—this stranger! She felt her own inadequacy acutely, turning her eyes from Burke's quizzing blue ones. "I—I hope I don't disappoint you," she mumbled—and felt desperately like a greenhorn typist mumbling to her new boss: "I hope I give satisfaction."

Again Burke bent over her, turning her face to him with a gentle hand. His smile now was grave. "Everything's going to be fine, little one. Now go to sleep. Goodnight." He left her then, moving away into the shadows, quietly letting himself out of the room.

And somewhat reassured, Rea curled herself into a warm little ball and drifted into sleep.

CHAPTER FIVE

IT was Peter who woke Rea, woke her from deep, lost sleep, in the great bed. She sat up, startled, not quite knowing where she was for a second or two. Then Peter gave another lusty yell and Rea came completely awake to her surroundings. She scrambled from the bed and stood shivering in the early morning cold, lifting the crying baby from his cradle. She studied his red and angry little face with concern, the great tears sliding down his cheeks. "What is it, Petey boy?" she whispered. "Oh, I do wish you could talk, darling. I do wish you could tell me what to do. I'm a poor sort of a mother for you, aren't I? Are you hungry, then?"

He gulped on a sob, choked a little, and Rea's anxious heart came into her throat.

Would Moira be up? Moira would know what to do!

Hurriedly Rea laid the baby back in his cradle and scrambled into her dressing-gown and slippers. Then she took him up once more, wrapped him in his blanket and carried him from the room. She stood in the quiet corridor, gazing right, then left. How did one get to the kitchen? She took half a dozen tentative steps along the landing, pleading quietly, worriedly with the sobbing Peter. Everything was so quiet! And the light beyond the oriel window she was approaching was still the pale grey of very early morning.

Then, almost at her elbow, a door opened. Rea stood petrified, gazing at the silver-haired figure of the master of King's Beeches. The white bars of his eyebrows were drawn down in a heavy frown, and his tall, bony frame, enveloped in a claret-coloured dressing-gown, was taut with harsh surprise.

"That youngster's making a damnable racket, miss!" He stamped across to her and stood over her, his eyes gimlet hard. "What's up with him, then?"

"He's—he's hungry, I think." Rea—she couldn't help herself—was terrified of the old, angry man. "I was going to the kitchen . . . I thought someone might be there."

"There's a bell in your room, miss," the old man snapped. "Go back and ring it. One of the girls will come up to you." Then he turned and went back into his room and Rea jumped as the door snapped shut.

With burning cheeks and a throat that felt full of tears, Rea returned to her bedroom. She located the bell and pressed it and within minutes the brisk, brown-eyed Moira was bustling into the room.

Her "Good mornin', ma'am!" was respectful enough, but her smile was inclined to be inquisitive. Down in the kitchen last night she had said to Tolliver: " 'Tis a joke the young master must be playing, Mr. Tolliver. He isn't truly wedded to such a tiny, scrawny bit, now is he?"

"They've a babe to prove it," Tolliver—who was less impassive in the kitchen—had retorted.

Now Moira took that same babe in her strong brown arms. "My, but he is in a paddy, ma'am!" she exclaimed, and the glance she cast at Rea plainly intimated that she thought her every bit as inadequate as Rea knew herself to be. Then Moira, seeing the blush that stole over the pale face of Rea, framed in the fine, straight, child's hair, said with more kindliness: "I'll take him down with me and see to him, ma'am, don't you fret. T'young master said last night that I was to help you all I could with your baby."

"You're very kind." Rea's smile was hesitant, for she was frankly intimidated by the very efficient Moira, with her glance that didn't trouble to hide its unflattering summing up of herself.

"I'm happy to be that, ma'am." Moira gave a little bob, and then marched briskly to the door, carrying the baby off with a proprietorial air. Just before she closed the door, she said to Rea: "Early tea will be up in five minutes or so, ma'am."

The door closed and Rea was left alone in the big bedroom, still lit by the low glimmer of the oil-lamp she had not extinguished the night before. It gave the room a dull, yellow look, clashing with the thin bars of sunshine now striking through the curtains at the windows. Rea extinguished the lamp and drew the curtains open. The stableyard below was a-flutter with brown and white hens, running before the inquisitive noses of two big dogs. And beyond the wall of the stable-yard a meadow, swathed in a slight mist, stretched to the dense, still green of a wood, above whose tall trees birds wheeled and dived in an abandon of early morning joy.

Rea's spirits began to revive. There was beauty here, and friendly animal sounds that she couldn't help but respond to. And later on in the day, if she wished, she could wander in that meadow, make her way down into the green heart of that wood. She was no longer tied to the tedious wheel of employment—she was free!

Came a tap at the door and she became guiltily still. She was smoothing her hair when the door opened and a maid appeared with her early tea. This girl was less bustling than the rather familiar Moira, but none the less curious. Her eyes, under a cap worn rather low down on her forehead, stared at Rea as she set the tea-tray down on the bedside table.

Rea met the girl's look and suddenly knew a desire to exert her authority as Burke's wife; or at least to show that she wasn't quite the tongue-tied ninny everybody here seemed to be thinking her. "I hope Moira has managed to pacify my—my son," she said, coming to the bedside and helping herself to one of the biscuits the maid had brought with the tea. She bit into it, assuming a nonchalant attitude. "He's really a very good baby. I think the strange country noises frightened him."

The little maid gulped, twisted her hands in her apron and then nodded. " 'Tis very likely, ma'am," she said shyly.

Rea smiled at her. "What time is breakfast?" she asked.

"Half-past eight, ma'am." The girl hesitated at the door. "Was there anything else, ma'am?"

Rea took up her tea, stirring it rather quickly. "You—you might tell me how I get to the breakfast-room. This house is so vast—there are so many rooms!"

The maid's eyes flew wide open. "Why, ma'am, 'tis the first door to your right as you go down the stairs—the stairs on the left-hand side of the hall, that is."

"Thank you." Rea's smile was half impish, half self-disparaging as she sipped her tea and watched the little maid go scuttling away. Doubtless she would inform the other members of the kitchen that she had had to give the new mistress directions on how to get to the breakfast-room. And doubtless there would be amused comment. "My, but she's the quaint one," someone would say. "How come young master married her?" And very likely Moira, that self-assured young creature, would hold Peter high in her arms and her knowing laughter would fill the kitchen!

Burke didn't appear for breakfast and Rea felt very shy and uncertain sitting alone with his grandfather. He ate very little, studiedly ignoring her from behind a rattling newspaper, and though Rea longed to ask him where Burke might be, she didn't dare.

The room they sat in had tall glass doors opening on to a terrace, where a great brown and black Alsatian dog was prowling. Every now and again he would pause in his prowling, peer in through the glass of the closed doors and yelp at his master, immersed so irritably in the morning paper. Rea watched the dog, smiling slightly as he lifted a paw and impatiently tapped upon the glass. He had a saucy, handsome face, with a big ruff about his neck and alertly cocked ears, and as he again tapped upon the glass, Burke's grandfather turned sharply in his chair. "Be quiet, you old fool!" he ordered. The dog yelped in answer, his head slowly going over on one side.

"What's his name?" Rea asked shyly.

The old man rattled his newspaper, seeming to debate whether to answer her or not. Rea bit her lip, feeling his hostility so acutely that she wanted to leap from her chair and go running from the room.

"His name is Rafe," Mr. Ryeland said at last, curtly. "But beware of him, miss. He looks friendly, but he won't countenance any pretty pettings and pattings—

he hasn't been reared to them." Abruply he laid aside his newspaper. "That husband of yours, if you're interested, has gone off to do a bit of surveying for me and won't be back until this afternoon. He said something about some nursery furniture coming along from Taunton and he wants it put in the room he and his brother used to share when they were children. Get one of the maids to show it to you, you may want to clear some of the old stuff out of it."

She nodded, flushing under the old man's gimlet stare.

"It's incredible!" he suddenly grunted, his cold blue eyes sweeping her from head to foot, scornful assessing, contemptuously dismissing. "The boy's done it for a damn joke!" Then he rose, walked with stiff, fiercely offended pride to the glass doors and let himself out on to the terrace, where the big dog frisked around him like a puppy, eagerly following him down the stone steps and across the lawn.

Rea sat forlornly at the table, nervously jumping when Tolliver came soundlessly into the room. She watched his impassive back as he busied himself at the sideboard. "Tolliver," she spoke tentatively, but he turned at once, presenting a polite face. "Tolliver, when you return to the kitchen will you tell Moira that I want to see her. I want her to help me clear out my—my husband's old nursery. A batch of new furniture has been ordered from Taunton and will probably arrive here some time today."

"Yes, madam." He hesitated a moment, then a slight, surprising smile lit his rather saturnine face. "It's a pleasant feeling, madam, having a child in the house, if you don't mind my saying so. We in the servants' hall are quite delighted."

"Really, Tolliver?" Rea's smile was warm with surprise at this overture. Then with a rush she said: "Have you been with the family a good many years?"

And the young wistfulness of her face, the unconscious revealing of how little she knew of her husband's family, moved Tolliver to a sympathetic expansiveness —and the thought that Mr. Burke had brought back many a strange curio from his travels, but never a stranger one than this small wife, complete with a handsome Ryeland baby. "Since I was a young man, madam," he said, "when the two boys were still very young. Their mother died when Mr. Philip was born. They were fine boys, madam, though Mr. Philip was always the quieter of the two. Master Peter has a look of his uncle, I think."

"Has he, Tolliver?" Rea examined the butler's polite face, a moment of panic sweeping through her. "Were my husband and his brother not alike to look at, then?"

"Only about the eyes, madam. Mr. Philip resembled his grandmother."

"I see." Rea took up a fork and made patterns on the tablecloth. "His death must have hurt Mr. Ryeland a great deal. My husband says they were very attached to one another."

"Yes, indeed, madam! Mr. Philip always took such a pride in King's Beeches, you see, right from a boy."

"It is a beautiful house, isn't it, Tolliver? And so big! I know I shall get lost, again and again." Rea's smile was slightly rueful as she laid down the fork and rose to her feet. "I'm holding up your work, Tolliver, sitting about here. You will send Moira to me, won't you? I'll be in the garden."

He inclined his head, stepping to the glass doors and holding them open for Rea. She made her way down into the garden, where the sun had grown a little warmer, spreading across the lawn and bringing to glowing life the scarlet of salvias, the reddish-purple of hydrangeas, the massed rainbow tints of a great bank of chrysanthemums.

Rea stood by the sundial in the middle of the lawn, tracing out the inscription with her forefinger. "Time walks before me and Fate treads my heels," she read. She smiled, in a wistful, slightly hurt fashion. She felt as though the very open contempt and dislike of old Philip Ryeland were treading her heels, casting their shadow over this new life she had undertaken. It was only in Burke's tall presence that she knew a lessening of tension, a small measure of confidence, but once cut off from him, she became a ridiculous intruder in this house. Regarded with amused incredibility by the servants and dismissed as a hateful joke by the master!

Yet without the shyness and the self-effacement they so scorned, she wouldn't be here. They were the attributes Burke liked. He had made her Mrs. Burke Ryeland of King's Beeches, but he knew she would never presume on her position; she was, and would continue to be, Rea Glyn, the little shy typist he had met in a seaside hotel.

Suddenly she became aware of somebody standing behind her. She swung round, and found herself gazing at a tall, wonderfully built girl in khaki riding-breeches and a dark green, high-necked sweater. Her hair, which was a glistening chestnut, was cut close to her head, but it in no way gave her a masculine appearance. She wasn't exactly beautiful, but her tanned features were undeniably striking, possessed of that self-assured haughtiness that so distinguished Burke and his grandfather.

The girl was frankly examining Rea, negligently swinging a riding-switch against the side of her leg as she did so. "Who the devil are you?" she suddenly asked, in a deep, clipped voice.

"I—I'm Rea Glyn." Then Rea remembered and a vivid blush mounted into her face. "I mean—I'm Burke's wife. We—we only came last night."

"Good God!" The girl drew closer to Rea and her dark, jade-green eyes expressed a flash of shock that was almost immediately replaced by a gleam of arrogant, confident laughter. "Come off it. Burke wouldn't marry a baby like you!"

"Well—well, he did." Rea stood small and childlike before this handsome creature, her fair fringe tossed by the wind that was coming across the garden, bringing with it the green tang of high and open places. She looked about sixteen, and pale to the point of being washed out. She hadn't an ounce of assurance to set against the flaunting vividness of the girl before her; she felt ridiculous, laughable, naming herself Burke's wife. She wanted, suddenly, to go sinking through the close-cut grass at her feet. Here, she knew, in one sweeping moment of revelation, stood the girl Polly Wilmot had referred to—the girl Burke's grandfather had wished him to marry. Here she stood, pagan and proud, chestnut hair gleaming in the sunshine, chiselled features taut with scorn and dismissal.

"Burke likes his little joke, I know," came the clipped, contemptuous voice, "but he was never one to subscribe to a farce. You've thought this little farce up on your own—Miss Whoever-you-are."

And then, in a brisk, solid fashion Rea couldn't help but appreciate, Moira, the maid, added her brisk, solid person to the scene. She came out upon the lawn with little Peter in her arms and as she approached Rea, she said, with a broad smile: "T' baby can't wait to get to you, ma'am, see how he fights me?"

Rea, with eyes that were suddenly sparkling, took the baby close to her. She turned in a quiet triumph to the girl in breeches. "Burke's son," she said, quite calmly, pulling the shawl away from the baby's face. "He's rather nice, don't you think?"

"Burke's son!" The girl gaped at the gurgling baby, with his very blue eyes, his saucily dimpled chin, and his button of a nose pushed into wrinkles as he fought to take possession of a little black velvet bow at the neck of Rea's white blouse. "Burke's son!" The girl's voice rose almost upon a note of wildness. "I don't believe it!" She stepped close to Rea and her shocked eyes stared down at the baby, whose blue eyes drew away from Rea's bow and met, with solemnity, the hard, brilliant stare above him. He blinked once or twice, the feathery fans of his black lashes sweeping down and then lifting in a fashion that, if it remained with him as he grew older, would be thought highly flirtatious, but none the less endearing, by the ladies.

This tall girl, however, was in no mood to find little Peter endearing. "How old is he?" she demanded.

"Five months." Rea met the girl's eyes, full of wonder that she could discuss Peter in such a calm, proud manner—as though she were indeed his mother. Anyway, she felt like his mother, with his small, firm body pressing to her with that primitive, rather lovely eagerness of all young things to know the softness and the gentleness of the female body. His head arched back against her breast and he gazed up at her with his enormous eyes, and Rea laughed eagerly, no longer quite as afraid of the tall girl in the breeches as she had been.

"Do you—do you mean to tell me Burke has been married for well over a year?" The jade-green eyes flashed over Rea in an angry, wounded way. "Oh, no! I won't believe it! He wouldn't keep anything like that from me—he'd have told me! He—" She broke off, abruptly aware that Moira was standing respectfully to one side, awaiting Rea's pleasure. "What do you want?" she demanded of Moira, her voice rising high and sharp with the humiliating knowledge that the maid had heard what she had just said about Burke.

"Madam wishes me to help her prepare Master Peter's nursery, miss." Moira's eyes were lifted in a blank politeness to the tanned, angry face above her. "I'm waiting for madam to give me my orders."

"Oh!" The deep breast, under the dark green sweater, rose and fell quickly, and the riding-switch in the girl's hand beat regularly, agitatedly, against the side of her breeches. She stood a moment, glaring at Moira, then, with an extra hard thwack of the riding-switch, she swung on her booted heel and strode across the lawn, mounting the stone steps of the terrace and entering the house in the assured manner of someone who has had the run of the place for a good many years.

Rea shivered, as though suddenly cold. This girl, whoever she was, belonged to King's Beeches. She fitted into the grace and grandeur of the place; possessed the pride and the personality that would unfold glowingly in ancient panelled rooms. She wouldn't look, and feel, a pale shadow, an unwanted guest.

Rea said to Moira, almost whispering the words: "Who is she?"

"Miss Iris Mallory, ma'am, from Mallory Court, three miles over t'hill. She comes and she goes, like; she always has. T'old master has always made a lot of her."

"I—see." Rea stood gazing across at the terrace, at the half-open glass doors, through which Miss Iris

Mallory, of Mallory Court, had marched with such angry assurance. In every way the sort of girl Philip Ryeland would strongly desire for a granddaughter-in-law. Handsome and arrogant; bred to the life of a house like King's Beeches, and built to produce half a dozen lusty children. No wonder he looked at her, Rea, with such malevolent eyes. She symbolized his broken hopes; and she did more, she embodied all the qualities his hard, unyielding, despotic nature would be bound to despise: shyness in place of proud self-confidence, the lack of a lineage to match Burke's, a gentleness he would call callow meekness; instead of the strong, personal, sensual attraction that lay like a lush bloom over the tanned and statuesque Iris Mallory.

She glanced down at Peter, whose happy fist had now won a hold upon her black velvet bow and was busily tugging it from its cotton moorings. Surely the old man wouldn't include Peter in his hating—Peter was only a baby! Peter was the reason Burke had made his—his preposterous marriage. Peter was his gift to this house.

And then the tears she had fought on and off all the morning suddenly swam thick in her eyes. "Oh, Petey, I do love you!" she gasped.

The baby responded with a chuckle and a wriggle and a long, slow blink of his eyelashes, just as though he understood her words and wanted to reply that he, too, was feeling affectionate.

"Don't you think he's perfectly lovely, Moira?" Rea exclaimed, the tears spilling from her lashes even as she smiled her delight in the baby.

"Aye, he's ruddy and splendid as a September apple right enough, ma'am," Moira agreed, smiling upon Rea in an indulgent fashion. Ah, but it was nice, and there was no denying it, to see this wee bit of a thing so eaten up with her babe. There were no uppish town ways about her, which was a blessing. But she certainly was a funny sort of fancy for t'young master to be having. Thin as a switch and not much to look at—until she smiled.

Aye, when she smiled there was a sort of charm to the thin little face—a pixieish sort of charm in the way the huge hazel eyes went all crinkly and the cheekbones went slanting away from the soft young mouth and the delicately pointed chin. Maybe 'twas her smile t'young master had been caught by—and caught he evidently thought himself, from the way he had kept the whole business of his marriage so secret. A rather sly gleam darted in and out of Moira's brown eye. Miss Mallory would have plenty to say to him, no doubt! She, as everyone in the county knew, had confidently reckoned on being mistress of King's Beeches. But this bit of a girl, with her fringe and her baby, had swiped the prize.

Moira knew a stirring of profound admiration. There was more to this wee creature, she decided, than met the eye. Miss Mallory might be handsome and bold and a rare sight to see in the saddle and upon the ballroom floor, but she had let Master Burke give her the slip all right, straight into the arms of a lass who looked as though she'd lift and drift on a gusty bit of breeze like thistledown.

CHAPTER SIX

THE new nursery furniture, along with a wonderful zoo of enormous fluffy animals and a cream and brown perambulator, arrived from Taunton at two o'clock that afternoon. Rea and Moira then spent a couple of noisy hours arranging it in the big 'sunny' south room that had once been the nursery, and later the schoolroom, of Burke and his brother.

It was delightful pastel furniture, with golliwogs and teddy-bears and all manner of fairyland creatures painted all over it, and by the time it was set out to Rea's satisfaction the room had taken on an air of colour and enchantment, its old look of neglect quite banished.

"Nice, Moira?" Rea queried.

"Very nice, ma'am," and Moira smiled at the way Rea had curled herself down in the window seat, a big pink elephant in her lap and a judicious expression of satisfaction on her face as she gazed round the nursery. "Master Peter is a very lucky little boy, ma'am."

"Yes, Moira, very, very lucky," Rea said.

"Well, I'll be off to take t'baby for a blow round the garden in his new carriage, ma'am," Moira said, lingering a moment by the door for one more look round the nursery. A complacent gleam settled in her brown eyes. She had been elevated to the position of nursemaid and the thought was a very pleasing one. "Aye, 'tis a real pleasant nursery now, ma'am," she said, and her brown cheeks wore dimples as big as pennies as she hurried away to commence her new duties.

Rea knelt up in the window seat, cuddling the elephant in her arms and gazing out over the big garden. It was quiet and somnolent under a surprisingly warm autumn sun, the paved walks looking very clean and swept, the box-hedges prim and neat above the bright banks of flowers. Beyond the garden, below wide stone steps, Rea could see the velvety stretches of a bowling green, edged by tall silver birches. Rea thought the scene as calm and lovely as the centrepiece on a porcelain plate.

She was still sitting in the window seat, when the door swung open and Burke strolled into the room. He wore riding clothes, and seemed suddenly a stranger.

His dark virility, that ordinary clothing tempered down into a dark distinction, was released almost alarmingly now by the way his white shirt was thrown open at his bronzed throat; by the corded breeches and the heavy brown riding boots. His hair, too, was dishevelled from his riding where always before she had seen him immaculately brushed and combed.

He watched her for a second or two, as though expecting her to give him some word of greeting, but when she didn't one of his black brows rose in a quizzing fashion. He strolled across the room to her and stood looking down at her. "D'you like the toys, Rea?" he drawled.

She nodded jerkily, feeling her cheeks grow warm. She carefully set aside the pink elephant. "Peter will love them," she said. "They're like something out of fairyland."

"All successful toys should have that quality, Rea." His slow smile etched deep, attractive grooves in his brown cheeks. "Now what have you been doing with yourself all day? Have you made friends with Grandfather yet?"

She shook her head, smiling slightly. "Don't expect him to like me—how could he? It isn't in the nature of an eagle to welcome a sparrow into its eyrie."

"How about a dove?" Burke queried, and abruptly he reached for her hand and pulled her to her feet. "Come with me," he said, "there's something I'd like you to see."

He hurried her from the room, her hand held fast in his, marched her along the landing and ran her down the stairs. He crossed the hall with her and threw open the door of a room that made Rea's eyes open wide with admiration. But Burke gave her no chance to stand and stare, he took her straight across the silken rugs, with their glowing jewel colours, and stood her in front of the carved oak mantelpiece. Above the mantelpiece hung the Ryeland crest—a bold, peering dove preening its feathers on the richly decorated handle of the sword. Below the crest was sprawled the Latin inscription, "Fortes Fortuna Juvat."

"Do you know what it means, Rea?" Burke murmured.

" 'Fortune favours the brave.' " She laughed up at him. "I shall never, never preen my feathers on your grandfather's sword. It's too much to hope for. I'm not," she glanced down, biting her lip, "I'm not Iris Mallory, you see."

In a moment he had released her hand. As he stepped way from her, he swore slightly. He paused beside a low rosewood table and threw back the lid of a cigarette box. He selected a cigarette, lit it carefully. Then he said: "So you've now met the redoubtable Iris? I take it you were suitably impressed?"

"I thought her very handsome, naturally," Rea said.

He swung round, his blue eyes brilliant with what she took to be anger. "Listen to me, Rea," he said. "Contrary to what people will tell you, I've never given Iris Mallory any reason to think that I ever contemplated marrying her. I know my grandfather had hopes of such a marriage and very possibly that hope influenced Iris. I'm telling you this, Rea, because I don't want you to go jumping to the misguided conclusion that I've been playing fast and loose with Iris." He lifted his cigarette and drew hard upon it. "Only once in my life did I play that game—and lived to regret it"

He walked to the window and leaned his shoulder against the frame, his face suddenly moody as he gazed out upon the orchard, where red and gold apples gleamed through green leaves. "Do you think, Rea," he said, "that one ever stops paying for one's mistakes? Does God demand a lifetime of regret?"

His quiet, melancholy words seemed to pierce Rea. She watched his lounging figure, thrown into dark, vital relief by the gleaming ruby damask of the curtains at his shoulder, and she was moved to approach him, but shyness held her back. "Not if one's mistakes are genuine, I shouldn't think, Burke," she said.

"That's just the trouble," he turned his head and stared at her. "My mistake wasn't a genuine one." Then, with a shrug and a laugh, he threw off depression. He bent to undo the latch of the window where he stood and beckoned Rea to follow him out to the orchard. She did so, breathing the fragrant air with delight. The trees seemed to bend under their burdens of rich cider apples, shedding some of them into the grass, where they lay gleaming. Burke bent and picked one up, handing it to Rea. "For being a good girl," he smiled.

She tossed the sun-warmed apple in her two hands as she walked beside Burke through the orchard, and as he glanced down at her, prim as a schoolgirl in her white blouse and dark skirt, swinging above her long legs, he broke into a grin. "You look about fourteen," he said. "I think I'll buy you a tricycle and let you ride round the grounds on it."

"Oh, don't!" Her eyes opened wide at him. "I'm sure I'm the talk of the servants' hall already. Moira gives me the most peculiar looks."

"What sort of a look did Iris Mallory give you?"

A smile danced impishly upon the corners of Rea's mouth. "I believe she thought me an urchin who had strolled in from the village. She looked all prepared to take me by the scruff of the neck and bundle me out of the grounds. Moira saved the situation—she brought Peter to me."

"And the proof of the pudding very successfully whittled the lovely but haughty Iris down to size!" Burke's deep laughter rang through the orchard, startling a trio of birds out of one of the trees. "I'd like to have been there! Oh, there's no getting away from it, Rea, this situation definitely has its amusing side." His blue eyes danced as he paused under a tree and leant his wide back against it.

Rea stood tossing the golden apple. Burke might be amused, she thought, but the situation wasn't all that amusing for her. Philip Ryeland most emphatically did not like her, and there was every likelihood that Iris

Mallory, out of pique, would say things to him that might set him wondering; set him asking questions of Burke. Awkward questions. Questions about how they had met—where they had met. Rea ceased to toss the apple, her eyes growing wide and panicky. Was she expected to say that it was in Peru they had met? "I've never been to Peru—I know nothing about the place!" she gasped aloud.

"It's hot and primitive and it steams," Burke drawled. He watched her, amusedly, reading her panicky thoughts in her eyes. "We'll tell Iris I found you under a banyan tree, dressed in half a dozen inches of dyed grass."

"Oh, don't! I'd never live that down! What will you really tell her?"

"I'll tell her as much, or as little, as it suits me to tell her." Burke reached up a lazy hand and plucked a spray of apple leaves. He spun the spray in his fingers. "Don't be intimidated by Iris," he said. "She might be Grandfather's prize pet, but she knows I'll not tolerate any of her hankying about with anything that is mine." He passed an arm about her shoulders and walked her back under the trees towards the open glass doors of the drawing-room. "Iris is all right, really," he said. "She's just been rather spoiled by a doting father. Highly-strung fillies need a strong hand, and he's never used one."

Rea possessed only two dresses that approached, in her opinion, anywhere near the demands of sitting down to dinner under the gabled and turreted roof of King's Beeches. One was an old-rose colour, the other violet-blue. And both of them were in London, at the flat of Laura Damien.

So, for the second time, Rea sat down to dinner at King's Beeches in plain navy-blue linen.

She wouldn't have felt so acutely the inadequacy of her rather schoolgirlish dress if there had been no Iris Mallory, glowingly alive in a superbly cut dress of several shades of honey, with pearl studs in her ears, sitting across the table from her. She was so undeniably attractive, so smart and vivid, that Rea actually ached with the knowledge of how unattractive, dowdy and dull she must look in contrast.

She ate her dinner in a dull silence, constantly aware of Iris's jade-green eyes upon her, but they had reached the sweet course before Iris directly mentioned Burke's marriage, which had come as such a shock to her.

"I've met your son, Burke," she said, "did you know?"

He glanced up from his brandied pears. "Who do you think he resembles?" he drawled.

"You, of course, my dear." She smiled in a bitter-sweet fashion.

"Nonsense!" This expletive came from Philip Ryeland. "The boy is like my lad, like my Philip. Dead spit of him."

"Really?" The jade-green eyes opened very wide and then went gleamingly narrow. "I'll have to take another look at him."

"Yes, do that, Iris," Burke murmured. "Get Rea to take you up to the nursery after we've had dinner. You'll love his toys—he's got quite a young zoo up there, hasn't he, Rea?" Burke's blue eyes rested upon Rea's face, a lazy smile in them. "Show Iris the pink elephant, the one you like playing with."

"Oh, does she play with the baby's toys?" Iris laughed, softly. "How unutterably—comical."

"Yes, isn't it?" Burke took up his wine glass, the opaque stem looking very delicate in his brown hand. He sipped the wine, which had a pale golden sheen. "This has a pleasant softness, sir," he said to his grandfather. "Italian?"

The old man nodded. "Thought I'd try it, as Tab Gresham recommended it. Not bad, eh? One thing I'll say for Tab, he's got an unassailable palate, but like all doctors he plays a rotten game of bridge."

"You and your bridge!" Iris laughed and reached over to pat the old man's hand. "Well, there's four of us, we could make up a table tonight."

"I—I don't play—I'm awfully sorry!" Rea broke in.

"Don't be sorry, my darling." Burke's smile was

rakish. "I like you just the way you are, without any vices."

"Hasn't she one little one to make life exciting for you, Burke?" Iris laughed. Then she glanced at Rea, speculatively. "Do you ride?" she asked.

Rea shook her head. "There's—never been an opportunity to learn."

"How extraordinary! Burke lives in the saddle when he's here at King's Beeches." Her green glance swivelled to Burke. "Wherever did you find your wife, my dear—in a convent?"

Rea's heart seemed to turn a complete somersault at the question, while her eyes became fixed upon the dark, unconcerned-appearing face of Burke. She had hoped and prayed that they might elude this question and so avoid the lie that Burke must now tell; her young, honest heart shrank from that lie.

"Why, we met abroad," he said lazily. "Rea was playing secretary to some woman I knew. I rescued her." He smiled straight into Rea's eyes. "Eat your pears up, sweetie, then you can take Iris to see the baby." His smile moved to Iris. "You wouldn't think she had a baby, would you? She looks such a baby herself."

"Oh, I don't know," Iris retorted, with her bitter-sweet smile. "Dull covers often hide surprising literature."

"And vivid ones some surprising mediocrity," Burke returned swiftly.

Rea saw Iris go tense in her chair, while her cheeks definitely paled under the smooth tan. Why—why, she loves him, Rea thought, rather wildly. Burke knows she loves him and he doesn't care a jot. He doesn't feel that the minutest speck of love from anyone demands, at the least, gratitude. Rea shivered. So far Burke had shown her kindness, but what if he ever turned on her with his cutting tongue, lashing out and hurting for the mere pleasure of it? She shrank from the thought. He was her only friend in this new, strange world she had entered; he must stay her friend.

She covertly studied him as he talked now with his grandfather, discussing the piece of land he had been sent to survey that morning. She knew so little of him, and what she knew presented an enigma. Laura Damien had called him hard; she had held the opinion that he had never cared for anyone in his entire life. Yet Rea was convinced that in his own fashion he had loved Peter's mother. It wasn't because Peter was a Ryeland that Burke had brought him here to King's Beeches. It was because in some way he had hurt that girl Dani, and he made recompense by taking her son into the heart she had left empty.

Strange, complex heart, rejecting and yet observing, in its own puzzling fashion, its allegiance to this ancient house. Giving far more, really, than the brother who had died for it, for Philip had not died in bondage. Whereas Burke, whose eyes yearned for far horizons, would give the rest of his life to bondage!

Burke's remark had very successfully taken the sparkle out of the jewel-bright Iris. She was polite about Peter, fast asleep in his new nursery, apathetically amused by his collection of colourful toys, but very soon she turned to go. "Are you coming down?" she queried of Rea.

Rea shook her head. "I think I'll read a book," she said. "Please ask Mr. Ryeland and Burke to excuse me."

"Very well." Iris stood a moment by the door, gazing back at Rea, who had curled herself down in the padded window seat. She looked very young, the muted nursery light falling gently across her face and painting shadows in the slight hollows below her cheekbones. This twilight figure, of gentle muted tones and a youth that would be perennial, touched off the hate and resentment that had been simmering in Iris since the moment Rea had shyly introduced herself as Burke's wife. Burke's wife! Iris's green eyes lit to a catlike blaze and sudden quick words broke from her, so startling Rea that she curled into an even smaller figure in the window seat, her eyes growing large, her hands clenching together in her lap.

"You don't make the fantastic mistake of thinking Burke loves you, I hope?" Iris exclaimed. "He isn't capable of loving, you know! He wanted a son, that's all! He wanted a son, for King's Beeches—not a wife! And you're the perfect choice—placid, undemanding, giving him his son and then permitting him to tuck you away out of sight whenever he feels like it." Iris's full breasts lifted and fell stormily under the soft honey material of her dress. "I don't know whether you love him, but God help you if you do."

"God—help me?" Rea stared wide-eyed at Iris.

"Yes, God help you, for Burke Ryeland, you poor little innocent, takes a peculiar delight in breaking those who love him. He hates love, you see; it imprisons him—robs him of his precious freedom!" Her head went back and her chestnut hair gleamed angrily. "How he must hate Philip for dying—how he must hate you because he has had to marry and settle down here at King's Beeches. He *had* to marry, don't you see? That's how you got him."

With these words she was gone, the door closing sharply on the rich honey tones of her dress, a backwash of acute silence following the angry retreat of her high heels along the gallery.

Rea sat very still, caught trance-like in that queer web of following silence, her heart racing and thudding. She was learning so much of Burke tonight—too much—and she was afraid.

A little later Moira came up to bed. She was to sleep in the little room that led out from the nursery and Rea envied her. Her own room was so vast, so darkly grand, so full of shadows that the oil-lamps seemed unable to penetrate, but after she had said goodnight to Moira, she was reluctantly obliged to make her way to that room.

She was curled among her pillows, absorbed in the adventures of her great hero, Sydney Carton, when fingers suddenly rapped her door and then opened it.

When Rea glanced up and saw Burke, the magic of forgetfulness fled from her eyes. "Oh—hullo!" She pushed nervously at her fringe. "I—I hope it was all right, my not coming down?"

"Why didn't you?" He came to the bed and reached lazily for her book. He stood glancing through it, idly noticing that the book was a Christmas present, inscribed to 'My dear daughter.' "Did Iris frighten you?"

"Oh, no!" She shook her head. "I wanted to stay with Peter, that's all. I—I like him, you see. He's so little and sweet."

"And with him you feel safe," Burke added. "He can't ask questions, can he?" He shot her a quizzical look. "You nearly died, I saw it, when Iris wanted to know where we had met. Did she broach the subject again when you came up to see Peter?"

"No." Rea flushed, remembering what Iris had said, and Burke saw the flush, saw it stain her throat and mount into her cheeks. He bent and tipped up her chin with a gentle finger. "Suddenly you seem afraid," he said. "Are you afraid of me, Rea?" His eyes insistently searched her, held her, drew out her secret. "I see," he said at last, and his smile was whimsical. "Don't be afraid of me, Rea. I'd no more think of hurting you than I'd think of hurting Peter. You two are my family now, you know."

"Are we?" Her eyes were large on his dark, quizzical face. "You think of me like—like a daughter?" A strange hope, a bated, almost desperate hope edged her question, while her heart, under the blue linen of her pyjamas, beat with sudden nervous thumps.

His eyes dilated with surprise at her question, and then grew soft as they travelled the young face, so hopefully raised to him. "Why yes, Rea, I suppose that's how I do regard you. Why not?" He laughed gently. "I'm certainly old enough to be your father, presuming I was precocious enough to take a wife at the age of seventeen."

Seventeen, she thought, watching him. What had he been like at seventeen? Surely, even then, he had been stamped with a cool maturity; an air of withdrawal, as though human contacts were fundamentally unnecessary to him? "Weren't you precocious, Burke?" she murmured, a smile of sudden impishness darting across her pale face, banishing for the moment its gravity and its slight look of fear.

He fingered his chin, his eyes quizzical as he reflected on her question. "You should ask my grandfather that," he said. "If I remember rightly, I was writing rather fiery articles for the school rag—I was slightly Bolshevik in those days—and got myself expelled. Grandfather wore a purple face for weeks afterwards. I was a blot on the family escutcheon from that time onwards. Yes, I suppose you could say I had precocious tendencies, Rea." He grinned as he glanced at the book in his hands. "Are you fond of reading?"

She nodded. "I love *A Tale of Two Cities*. It's my favourite out of all Dicken's books. Have you read it?"

He nodded and smiled. "The inimitable Sydney Carton is your great hero, eh?"

She lay back against her pillows ruffling her fringe in thought. "I always cry when the little seamstress asks him to hold her hand. Do you think that's silly?"

"You think me cynical, Rca?"

"I—I don't know." Again her fingers pulled at her fringe, as though she had solved the problem in some measure. "I think you're probably a bit of a mixture. Your approach to real life problems is cynical, but imaginative things appeal to you, don't they?"

"It's my writer's mind, Rea," he agreed.

"Why don't you write another book?" she asked, looking suddenly eager.

"No." He shook his head. "No, it wouldn't do, my dear. I'd get discontented with—well, with things as they are now. It's best this way. I've turned a page on the past." Abruptly he turned and took the oil-lamp from the bedside table and carried it to the chest of drawers. "You're to go to sleep, now," he said, "it's well past eleven o'clock. I'll leave your book here, beside the lamp. D'you want both lamps turned out?"

"No, only one." Her voice came rather small from the bed. "This room is so big and dark—"

"You baby!" he laughed softly, as he turned out one lamp and lowered the other to a glimmer. "Is that all right?"

"Yes, thank you."

"You'll sleep? You won't lie awake worrying?"

"No."

Slowly he strolled back to the bedside and straightened the lace quilt across her shoulders. "Tomorrow, you funny child, I'll take you out and show you a bit of Somerset." Suddenly he grinned broadly. "Want me to go and get that pink elephant for you? You can cuddle him in bed."

She pulled a face at him. "You were very mean, telling Iris I play with Peter's toys. I felt six inches high."

He answered with a deep spurt of laughter and made his way to the door. "Poor old Iris, she did look startled, didn't she? She'll be telling the county that I've taken my wife straight out of the crêche." He stood by the door, still laughing. "I'll have to buy you some shockingly sophisticated frocks, my dear, and restore you to normal height. We'll go shopping just as soon as I can spare the time. . . ." Then he was gone, the heavy door creaking shut behind him.

Rea lay watching the flickering tongues of rather weird shadows the glimmering oil-lamp cast up the walls of her room.

Her second night at King's Beeches! The end of a day crowded with new, strange impressions!

There was Burke's grandfather, watching her at breakfast and suddenly exclaiming: "It's incredible! The boy's done it for a damn joke!" Rea's bottom lip trembled slightly and she swiftly caught it in her teeth, biting on it. It wasn't pleasant to be thought a joke, but she did see how she must look to him, beside the assured and picturesque Iris Mallory. A dull little nobody, who couldn't boast a single attraction—least of all, he must think, for a man like Burke, who had had the world to choose from, yet who had chosen to bring her here to King's Beeches as his wife.

Burke's wife! It was laughable!

But Iris Mallory hadn't laughed. Rea's toes curled nervously into the soft mound of the feather mattress. The lush Iris had been wildly jealous, her cat-green eyes tormented, her long nails barely held in control as she had faced Rea in the nursery, kneading and clenching the honey skirts of the dress that blended so well with the honey skin of her arms and throat. "Burke takes a peculiar delight in breaking those who love him!" she had cried.

And that, Rea thought, knowing it to be the complete and dismal and still rather frightening truth, was what he had done to Dani Larchmont.

CHAPTER SEVEN

SEPTEMBER turned the corner into October and suddenly it rained so hard some evenings that great puddles collected between the uneven kidney stones of the stable-yard and the rain splashed down the wide chimneys of King's Beeches and hissed as it died among the glowing apple logs.

It was very pleasant, Rea found, on such evenings as these, to spend the time curled up with a book in Burke's study, a room furnished with all the individuality of the lettered traveller Burke still was at heart, despite the farming tweed and the high brown boots he now wore six days out of seven; despite the businesslike manner in which he had taken control of all the Ryeland holdings.

He did a lot of his paper work here. "Farming," he ruefully told Rea, "might be a whole lot easier on the muscles these days, but there's a darned sight more red tape attached to it. Forms—forms! Look at these!"

So, while Burke filled in his forms, Rea either read to herself or she brought Peter and some of his toys down from the nursery and had an hour's game with him on the big Bokhara rug in front of the fireplace.

One evening Burke said to her: "You're getting a bit more used to the life here, aren't you, Rea?"

She nodded—but she knew in her heart that she was only released from real care when she played like this in this room that seemed miles from King's Beeches when the curtains were pulled on the ridge of the Mendips and the door safely shut and not likely to be opened by Burke's grandfather.

He never came here. He seemed to realize, and to be angered by the fact that the room had been deliberately designed by Burke as an escape valve.

And then, one morning, he did come.

Rafe, the big Alsatian, was with him, for the two were inseparable.

The big dog, rather to its master's annoyance, had taken a fancy to Rea; but the old man remained coldly hostile. Abruptly he said: "I hear you were up all last night with the boy. Got a cold or something, hasn't he?"

Rea nodded. "His teeth are coming through, you see. I hope we didn't disturb you?"

"No, no!" He shook his head. "It did occur to me, though, that it might be a good idea to have Tab Gresham over to see him. We don't want the lad sickening for anything."

Now Rea's hands fell idle as she gazed up at old Mr. Ryeland. So, behind that frozen face of indifference he invariably presented, even when he visited the nursery, he did care about Peter! She knew a warm rush of relief—of gratitude, almost. "To tell you the truth," she said, the words tumbling out of her mouth, "I should like Dr. Gresham to see him. I—I'm awfully glad you suggested it. Being such a plump baby, he could develop bronchitis. I don't want that to happen."

"No, no!" he said at once. "No, we certainly don't want that. As you say, he's a plump baby." He cleared his throat. "I'll send one of the servants over to Tab with a note." He shot her a sharp glance. "What did Burke think? Didn't he think the lad ought to have a doctor?"

"He said he'd call Dr. Gresham in if Peter didn't seem any better by lunchtime."

"Well, we'll get Tab now. I'll send over a note." For a moment he glared at her, as though she offended him, then he turned about and went stamping from the room. In a moment Rafe had scrambled to his feet and followed him.

Tab Gresham came within the hour.

He surprised Rea. Because Burke's grandfather was so friendly with him, she had expected him to be a middle-aged man. But he was round about Burke's age. A slender, sandy-haired man, with shrewd, grey-blue eyes and a jagged little half-moon scar immediately under his left cheekbone. He was the kind of person who is strongly likeable at first glance; an uncomplicated obviously dependable type.

He shook Rea's hand with warmth and as they went up the stairs to the nursery, he said: "I should have been over long before this to meet you, Mrs. Ryeland, but I've been playing lazy for the last three weeks. I've been up in Scotland, fishing."

"Then you're a traitor," Rea smiled. "Burke declares that the best fishing in England is to be found in the Barle."

"Ah, yes, but Burke is a Somerset man. I'm a Scot, Mrs. Ryeland."

"Oh, I see. Then that obviously excuses you," Rea met his smile with a lack of shyness that amazed her. Usually she found it difficult, this business of making ready conversation with a stranger. Always in the old days, her days with Mrs. Damien, she had found it difficult. Of course, Laura's friends had been rather different from this man—racy, aggressive, challenging her shyness rather than accepting it as part of her, like the colour of her eyes or the texture of her hair.

They went into the big colourful nursery. Moira was sitting with the fretful Peter, attempting to amuse him with one of his many toys, a dancing monkey in a straw hat. Usually he loved to watch this particular toy, but today he only lay grizzling, his sore gums sucking at his dimpled fists and his big blue eyes full of misery.

Tab Gresham immediately set about examining the baby, remarking to Rea: "He's very splendid, Mrs. Ryeland. What does his great-grandfather think of him?" Then he chuckled. "Adores him, I bet? Who wouldn't!" The long, sensitive hands, gently pressed the baby's neck glands. "Um, he seems to be teething with a sore throat and a slight earache, poor little feller."

"His chest is all right isn't it?" Rea queried anxiously.

Tab Gresham nodded reassuringly. "That huskiness you can hear is caused by the throat soreness. I've something to ease that. Mr. Ryeland's note mentioned that the baby was teething, so I took the precaution of bringing along with me a certain little mixture I recommend for this particular trouble. I'll give him a dose now."

"Is it nasty?" Rea watched him go to his medicine-bag, her hand stroking Peter's soft black curls.

Tab laughed. She was a nice child. She really was! "It isn't at all nasty, I assure you," he replied. "I wouldn't dream of giving *your* baby anything nasty."

By the time they went downstairs, luncheon was almost upon the table and Rea pressed Tab Gresham to stay and have some. "Thank you, Mrs. Ryeland, I'd love to," he said, and gave her that smile which sent his half-moon of a scar riding up upon his cheekbone.

Rea, with the doctor and Burke's grandfather, had only been at the table a few minutes when Burke joined them. He had been over at Shepton Mallet all the morning, conducting the sale of produce from one of the estate farms. Now, although he had obviously been upstairs to have a quick wash, he still looked rather heated, a lock of his black hair falling forward over one eye.

"Hullo, Tab!" He gave the doctor a broad grin. "Have you been up to see my boy? Is he all right?"

Tab nodded. "It's his teeth, Burke. He's cutting them with a slight throat and ear trouble. But I've given Mrs. Ryeland some medicine for him. He should be as bright as a new penny in a day or two."

"That's a relief!" Burke grinned at Tab. "Doesn't he make you feel like taking a pattern? You're getting on, boy, you should be thinking of settling down."

Tab's grey-blue eyes shot wide open. "I never thought I'd live to hear you say that, you darn Livingstone, you!" He turned his smile on Rea. "You've performed a miracle, young lady; are you aware of the fact?"

But Rea's answering smile wasn't truly spontaneous. She knew—she was the only one who knew—the desperate game of make-believe Burke was playing. . . .

"So the little lad has nothing seriously amiss with him?" Burke's grandfather broke in.

"Nothing that a good easy sleep won't put right, sir."

"He's—humph—he's a likely lad, eh, Tab?" The silver eyebrows shot rapidly up and down as old Mr. Ryeland helped himself to beef.

"No doubt about it, sir. He's built for any emergency, like his father."

Burke glanced up from his plate. His smile was quizzical. "You make me sound like a stevedore, Tab, old man. I resent the implication. You've got to remember that I'm a retired poet, traveller and writer."

His grandfather snorted, while Rea said with a shy eagerness: "I've been trying to persuade Burke to write another book, Dr. Gresham. I could take his dictation and do his typing. It used to be my job."

"What a splendid idea!" Tab exclaimed. "Now come on, Burke, don't let your talents go to seed. I know you're a farmer now, but as a farmer you should deplore the thought of anything going to waste."

"That's what I say," Rea agreed. "His field of imagination is lying fallow, and if he leaves it too long it will start growing stones and weeds."

Burke's deep laughter broke from his throat. "I'll leave it another year or two and it will start growing turnips."

"Burke, don't talk like that!" Rea exclaimed, hurt by the cynicism in his eyes.

"The boy's right," Mr. Ryeland grunted. "He's a farmer now. He's forgotten all that dashed literary nonsense." He cast a glare of frank irritation at Rea. "Remember it, will you, miss, and stop pestering him."

She flushed deeply. "But it isn't fair—he—"

"Stop it, miss!" The old man's fist came down hard upon the table, making the dishes and the glasses jump. "We'll hear no more of this puling foolishness!"

Burke glanced up the table sharply, a sudden flare to his nostrils, the lazy, rather cynical good humour wiped in a second from his sapphire eyes. "There's no need to speak to Rea in that tone, sir." He spoke crisply. "That puling foolishness, as you call it, still happens to mean quite a lot to me, though I've now put it out of my life. I'm grateful to Rea for her offer, even though I can't accept it."

"Really?" The old man glared down the shining table, with its lace mats, glittering Waterford glass and silver bowl of greenhouse lilies. "And do you think I'm grateful—grateful that you've always set out to do everything you knew would displease me?"

Burke's wide shoulders lifted in a shrug. "If our sympathies, our aims, our likes and dislikes, have always been in opposition, it hasn't been deliberate on my part, believe me, sir. I had to go my way, just as Phil had to go his. And if his way was yours, I don't suppose that was deliberate either."

"Don't talk of Philip!" The words came with a roar. "Philip was everything you could never be. He gave more than the sinews you now give to this house, he gave his heart and then his blood." With a harsh scrape upon the polished black oak floor, Mr. Ryeland's chair went back. He rose in trembling, white-faced anger to his feet. He addressed Dr. Gresham with harsh dignity: "Excuse me, Tab! It's uncouth to quarrel in front of guests and I'm well aware of the fact—but—dammit—" he threw out a hand that trembled towards Burke, "he never would listen to reason! Never!" Then he turned and went from the room. As the door slapped shut behind his elderly, offended figure, Burke drew a sigh.

"God, we don't outgrow our bad tempers, or our antagonism, he and I. I think, Tab, we must be constitutionally antipathetic, as you medical fellers would have it." Burke poured Richebourg with a rather unsteady hand. "The hell of it is, I'm tied here. I'm tied by my own damned conscience." His smile, over the rim of his glass, was cynical to the point of sheer melancholy. "You weren't aware that I had a conscience, were you, Tab? Well, I have. Like Jack's beanstalk it grew and it grew, and now it's so hardy that if I try to cut it down it will only send out new shoots."

He walked round the table to Rea and bent to her, holding her slim shoulders in his large, cool hands. "Stop looking as though you've brought all the gables and turrets of King's Beeches down on my head." His soft laughter moved her fringe. "We've always quarrelled, he and I. It's nothing to worry about."

"I—I can't help worrying!" She turned in agitation to him, meeting the deep, smiling blue eyes. "It isn't fair that he should think you—what you're not. It isn't fair!"

"We're never fair, Rea, or reasonable, when we lose what we cherish and continue to possess that which we despise. It's as simple as that, my dear. As simple and as cruel as that."

Though the afternoon was gusty and a trifle grey, Rea decided to take a walk. That sharp little exchange at luncheon had depressed her and she knew an almost desperate desire to escape from King's Beeches for an hour or two.

So, after she had bade Dr. Gresham goodbye and assured herself that Peter was peacefully sleeping, she hurried into her camel-hair coat and made her way out of the house, and down to the wood that lay at the bottom of the meadow.

She climbed the gate, jumped down upon dead furze stems, and entered the eerie, blue-green stillness of the wood. Great beeches arched their branches in a chancel-like formality high above her head, and then appeared the dull red trunks of slender larches, the sombre jade of elms, the solidity of lichen-draped oaks, with their branches flung out like beckoning arms.

It was about twenty minutes later that the trees thinned and the gloom lifed and Rea found herself standing at the foot of a winding lane, where the swollen, over-ripe faces of blackberries still gleamed in the tangled hedgerows.

The lane wound upwards, but Rea knew that the quickened beating of her heart wasn't due to the effort of mounting the lane; her legs were so long and young that they barely noticed the ground's elevation. It was apprehension that was hurrying her heart, the strange conviction that something was urging her to follow this lonely, wayside path.

Then, almost before she realised it, the lane had branched sharply to the right and she found herself gazing at a white door in a yew hedge that surely rose to a height of thirty feet. She slowly moved towards the door, nervously eager, urged by more than the Paul Pry instinct that a sudden and mysterious-looking door might arouse in the casual passer-by. She had come here as though called and she knew she must open this door.

She did so, her fingers shaking slightly on the latch, and the door swung open with an ease that testified to frequent oiling. She stepped through the door, on to uneven paving-stones that ran all the way round a green fronting an ancient black and white farmhouse. Three magnificent walnut trees stood in a triangle upon the green, and the roof of the farmhouse clustered with Tudor chimneys. There was a curious charm to the place; a lost and lonely charm, catching at Rea's heart, holding her transfixed by the white door. The moments sped as she stared, and when, with a sudden rush of guilt, she turned to dart away, a voice called out: "Hold hard, missie! Hold hard, now! Don't you be runnin' off!"

She gasped and stood in startled trepidation, watching a stocky, grey-haired man, with a bull-terrier at his heels, emerge from behind one of the massive walnut trees. He came across the green with heavy, deliberate strides. As he drew near to her, he said: " 'Tis private property ye're on, missie," and the bull-terrier, as though to add weight to the words, came to Rea's heels and gave a low, ominous growl.

"I'm—I'm awfully sorry I came through your door!" Rea gasped. "I—I wasn't thinking."

" 'Tis a dangerous habit, that, missie, not thinking before you act. If Mike here had been prowling about on his own, he'd have rushed you, taken some of your leg, like as not." Unsmiling, but not totally unfriendly eyes scanned her from head to foot. "Ah, I'm thinkin' I know you, missie. Ye're the lass from King's Beeches, aren't you? Seen ye before, I have, riding in that car of the young master's."

Her head gave a nervous little jerk of confirmation. "Yes, I'm Mrs. Ryeland," she said.

"Ah!" The man's lips became thoughtfully pursed in the deeply lined, weather-darkened face. Then abruptly, his gruffness gave way to a friendliness that was almost shy. "I wonder, missie, now you're here, would you take a cup of tea with my missus? Gets very few visitors, does my poor old girl. Y'see, she's an invalid. People," he shrugged heavily, "they don't seem to take much to invalids. 'Tis human nature to be that way, I suppose, but it makes my house a lonely one." Abruptly he smiled and held out a hand to Rea. "I'm James Larchmont, missie, one of old Mr. Ryeland's tenants."

Rea put her small hand into the big, warm hand of James Larchmont, lighting his rather weary eyes to a momentary brightness by saying: "I'd very much like to take a cup of tea with your wife, Mr. Larchmont."

"Then will you come this way, missie?"

They passed beyond the trees and crossed the uneven paving-stones to the front door of the farmhouse. A heavy, horseshoe-shaped door gave a deep creak as James Larchmont pushed it open, motioning Rea to precede him into a stone-flagged passage. At once she was aware of a strange chilliness; it came sweeping down the passage, along with a deadly stillness—and Rea knew that something frightening, something sad, something she would regret seeing, awaited her in this house. She stood stock still. "Are you sure—your wife won't mind?" she whispered.

"I'm very sure, missie." He spoke gently, realizing her moment of misgiving, seeing it written plain in her large rather frightened eyes. "Come straight along with me, missie, and don't be nervous. 'Tis a wee, pretty, harmless creature my missus is, though she can't rise to her feet and walk like you and me." And as he ceased to speak, he threw open a door and Rea found herself upon the threshold of a long, low-beamed room, with latticed windows draped with a flowered chintz; delicate, needlepoint chairs and footstools, and the recumbent form of a silver-haired woman upon a low, rose-coloured couch.

And even as the thought registered with Rea that this woman had once been very pretty, her eyes had gone beyond the delicate, tired face lifting in such wondering surprise to her, and had settled upon a face that laughed from a portrait above the fireplace. An exquisite, gipsy-wild, perfectly heart-shaped face, set with reckless dark eyes and framed in a riot of blue-black curls.

Rea felt her heart turn over. She had known there could be such beauty, but she had never before seen it. And she knew to whom it had belonged—she knew—she knew!

CHAPTER EIGHT

"I'VE brought you a visitor, my dear," James Larchmont said, gently propelling Rea across the room to the couch where his wife lay. " 'Tis young Mrs. Ryeland, from King's Beeches."

"Mrs.—Ryeland?" The faded blue eyes were fixed upon Rea in a childlike surprise. Then she said: "Of course, I remember Jim saying that Philip had married. How nice for him!" She turned her gentle, rather lost eyes to her husband. "Bring forward a chair for Mrs. Ryeland, Jim. Don't let her stand. I know she has had a long walk."

"I—I came through the wood," Rea said, speaking rather breathlessly. "It didn't take me so very long."

"Through the wood?" The gentle eyes slowly dilated. "But that isn't a nice place to be walking alone in, my dear. It is a dark, haunted place. You shouldn't—you really shouldn't have come that way."

"Oh, I didn't mind." Rea sank down into the low, needlepoint chair James Larchmont brought to the side of the couch. "There were only trees and birds and funny little bunches of toadstools and mushrooms growing under the trees."

"I never liked the wood." Mrs. Larchmont lifted her face to her husband. "I never liked it, did I, Jim? When I first came here as a bride, I would never go into it, would I?" Her glance returned to Rea and smiled. "Jim used to laugh like anything at my town ways—I was from London, you see." She reached out a tiny blue-veined hand and pressed Rea's wrist. "I believe you come from London, don't you, my dear?"

Rea nodded.

"How strange that Philip should marry a London girl—he with his passion for Somerset and all that it holds!"

"But I'm not married to—" then Rea broke off, for James Larchmont had closed a restraining hand upon her shoulder, his fingers pressing her to silence. She glanced up at him, rather wildly. But his face told her nothing; it was quite impassive.

"King's Beeches is a very beautiful house, isn't it?" the gentle, rather melancholy voice of Mrs. Larchmont continued. "How you must love living there, my dear. I always used to think of it as an enchanted house. Do you not think that it has that look? That untouched look, as of belonging in a world of its own?" She studied Rea, with her head a little to one side. "Yes, I can see that you love King's Beeches. Philip would want you to, he loves it so very much himself, doesn't he? Now his brother—I expect they've told you of him, haven't they?—he was so restless, so seeking; King's Beeches couldn't hold him. He went away, you know." She frowned and her glance slowly drew away from Rea's face. She ran a hand that trembled slightly through her silver curls. "Yes, he went away—they both went away."

"Both?" Rea's heart was beating high in her throat and once again she felt James Larchmont's fingers close upon her shoulder.

"Vera," he said, "I'm going to t'kitchen to make a pot of tea. I want you to show Mrs. Ryeland your lace-work. I'll fetch it, shall I?"

"Why—yes, Jim." Vera Larchmont gave him a child-like smile, a childlike compliance. "It's in the cabinet beside my bed. Mind you don't pull out any of my silks."

He strode from the room, and the dog, Mike, who had been sitting just inside the door as though reluctant to come farther, eagerly trotted out after him.

Silence fell upon the room. Mrs. Larchmont seemed to lose the desire for conversation, her eyes slowly turning to that laughing portrait above the fireplace, and Rea, watching her, suddenly saw her pretty wasted face take on the lax hopelessness of someone who waits—and waits in vain. Rea knew for whom she waited—knew that the girl in the portrait had been called Dani. So lovely—too lovely to be dead and alone!

Then Rea jumped, the awareness of a third person in that pretty but rather haunted room touching her like a cold finger. She turned a quick, startled head and met dark eyes so exactly like the eyes in the portrait that she knew this slender, insolently smiling man, hands thrust negligently in the pockets of very ancient breeches as he lounged in the doorway watching her, was Dani Larchmont's brother. She knew this as surely as though someone had told her; he had the same unruly blue-black hair and deeply dimpled chin, but what was gay daring in the girl's face was reckless insolence in the man's. He looked, Rea thought, exactly like a disreputable gipsy.

"A visitor, eh?" he said suddenly, pulling his shoulder away from the door and lounging into the room. Mrs. Larchmont drew her haunted eyes away from the laughing portrait of her daughter and slowly turned them upon the insolent face of her son. She stared at him as though she saw him through a mist. "Oh, is it you, Jack?" she said.

"Yes, Mother, it's Black Jack," he drawled. His eyes didn't leave Rea's face, and the smile that lifted one corner of his mouth in such a taunting, bitter fashion became slowly more pronounced as he crossed the room and stood over her. "The house of Larchmont is honoured—Mrs. Ryeland." The dark slanting eyes held Rea's in a glance that was almost mesmeric. "Let me introduce myself. I am Jack, scapegrace son of this very lovely lady here," he lightly touched his mother's shoulder, "and the earthy and estimable gentleman who is now carrying in tea." He swung round with the words and swept his father a low, mocking bow.

James Larchmont marched past him as though he wasn't there, lowered the tea-tray, with its quaint Staffordshire teapot and colourful cups and saucers, on to a table near his wife's couch. "Jack," he said, "I've left a mite of your mother's lacework in t'kitchen. Go and get it. It's on the dresser."

"With all speed, sir." Jack Larchmont sauntered to the door, but at the door he turned and once again Rea was treated to his insolent, half-smiling stare. It travelled over her, quite deliberately, then he turned and his booted heels rang loud on the stone flags of the passage as he made his way to the kitchen.

James Larchmont shot Rea a quick, rather embarrassed glance. "D'you take sugar, missie?" he asked.

Rea nodded. "Two lumps, please."

Then booted heels again rang on the stone flags outside and Jack Larchmont came back into the room. He brought the carefully rolled up piece of lacework to his mother and laid it in her lap. He grinned at her. "May the recalcitrant stay for a dish of tea Mother?" he queried.

But Mrs. Larchmont didn't answer, and Rea saw that she was nervously biting at her lip as she unwound the piece of lacework.

It was her husband who replied to Jack, bringing Rea's cup of tea to her and carefully placing it in her hand. "Hop it, Jack," he grunted. "Tea ain't your tipple, as I know. Hop round t'back and get the cows to the shed. 'Tis close on four."

"Perhaps Mrs. Ryeland wants me to stay," Jack drawled.

Rea glanced up at him, her cheeks growing pink. "I—I shouldn't dream of keeping you from your work, Mr. Larchmont," she exclaimed.

"Yet you could do it—so easily," he returned. His reckless, handsome face broke into a grin of taunting devilry. "You're banishing me to the cowshed, then?"

"Hop it, boy," James Larchmont said again. "Young missie ain't used to your manner of talkin'—she'll be takin' offence."

"Will you, young missie?" Jack raised an insolent eyebrow at Rea. "Will you be taking offence at poor Black Jack, when he means you no harm?"

Rea ducked her head away from his laughing eyes, taking an embarrassed gulp at her tea. With her eyes downcast, she shook her head in answer to his question.

She heard him laugh. Then, very deliberately, he went down on his haunches in front of her and thrust his face so close to hers that she could do nothing else but look at him.

"I'm terrible bad, little girl, as everyone hereabouts will eagerly tell you. I drink and I swear and I play when I should be milking the cows—but I'd like to be friends with you. May I be friends with you?"

"Of course, if you wish it," Rea stammered. She was painfully unnerved by him—and, at the same time, curiously excited to pity. Yet why should she feel pity for him? He looked the last person on earth in need of it. He had more than his share of good looks; he had obviously been well educated; and Rea knew, from the manner in which he addressed her, that he was a practised and recognized success with the ladies. Yet, gazing down into the reckless, slanting eyes, Rea felt an unmistakable pity for him touch her heart. The unhappiness that walked this house had not left this brother of Dani Larchmont's untouched. He might laugh it off, but it was at the heart of him, like canker at the heart of an outwardly sound-looking apple tree.

"You'll really be friends with me?" His eyebrows quirked at her in a half-mocking fashion. "You'll not be afraid of me, or turn the other cheek when I address you in the village?"

She shook her head. She even smiled slightly. "You don't look an ogre to me," she said.

"I hide my horns and my hoofs during the daylight hours, Mrs. Ryeland. We'll meet by moonlight sometime and you'll see me in my true guise." With these words he rose, reached a long arm to the sugar-bowl on the tea-tray beside his father, who was sipping tea in a rather morose fashion, and took about four lumps out of the bowl. He then went sauntering from the room, tossing the glistening cubes into his mouth and crunching them with his very white teeth.

With his going Mrs. Larchmont seemed to relax. She leant towards Rea, displaying her lacework, and Rea's eyes grew wide with admiration. This was genuine, delicate work, executed with great patience. "I made up the pattern myself," Mrs. Larchmont murmured.

"It's exquisite, it really is!" Rea said. "What wonderful patience you must have!"

"Vera has that, missie," James Larchmont said, pressing his wife's shoulder with a fond hand. "She's taught me to have it, bless her."

"Nonsense, Jim!" Mrs. Larchmont broke into a little trill of laughter. "That's nonsense," she said to Rea. "Jim is the soul of patience—and endurance. He has endured much, poor boy." The faded, lonely eyes stared straight into Rea's. "If you have found a love like the love my man gives me, then you have found great treasure." She pressed Rea's hand. "I like you, child. I think Philip is very lucky to have found you."

Half an hour later Rea walked with James Larchmont from the black and white farmhouse and as they crossed the green to the door in the yew hedge, he said: "I couldn't let you tell my missus that 'tis Mister Burke ye're wedded to. She wouldn't understand, y'see. Since she fell ill—'twas the death of our girl caused her illness—she gets muddled in her poor mind. But it does her such good to see a young creature like yourself, and I could see you wouldn't be foolish enough to be frightened by her. And you weren't, were you? She's such a poor thing, isn't she?" His question, put with such touching, prideful pathos, moved Rea to reach out and reassuringly press his arm.

"I thought her very lovely," she assured him. "Can—can nothing be done for her?"

He shook his head. " 'Twas a stroke, y'see. We never knew that our girl was ill, let alone dying, and the telegram came while I was out in t'fields. When I got home, my missus was as good as like a dead thing herself. I had to stay with her—I'd have lost her altogether if I had left her. And our girl—well, she was buried during that time I was tied to the bedside of my missus." He drew a harsh sigh and stared down at Rea—stared with a sudden searching intentness. "There's things we both know, Mrs. Ryeland—things that are best left unmentioned between us. But this I will say, I'm grateful to the heart of me for that certain responsibility your husband took upon himself that I, God help me, had neither the courage nor the charity to undertake."

"You—know?" Rea whispered.

His nod was heavy and slow. "Aye, I know that the child ye're rearing is my grandchild. I know, God help me again, that my Dani gave herself without love to young Philip Ryeland! Ah, well, 'tis done and can't be undone!" He swung open the white door and as Rea stepped into the quiet lane beyond it, he said: "Don't go through the wood, missie. It's not that there's anything amiss there but ye'll think of what my missus said and be nervous." He pointed along the lane, running beside the yew hedge as far as the eye could see. "Follow this lane, missie. It'll take you straight home."

"All right." She gave him her shy, charming smile. "Thank you for letting me meet your wife, Mr. Larchmont."

"Thank you for wanting to meet her, missie." He touched his cap, swung on his heel and disappeared through the white door. Rea started up the lane.

The wind had strengthened and a heavy chain of clouds was hurrying overhead, seeming to gather the fading daylight into them as they hurried. Rea pushed her hands into her pockets, walking forward into the wind, but unaware of it. How could Burke have hurt that lovely, lovely girl? she asked herself, unable to forget the blue-black curls, the small pout of a mouth, the tiny chin smudged with the same dimple that smudged Peter's chin. She had loved him! Laura Damien in fact had said that she had been crazy about him!

Rea touched the rain on her cheeks and the rain was cold and real as the knowledge that cruelty could lurk beneath Burke's smile, beneath all of his unfailing kindness to Peter and herself. Knowledge of his cruelty made his kindness less than it had been, for what did it cost him to be kind to—to a pair of babies? What, after all, did babies demand of a man? A few smiles. A few toys. A mere hour or two out of a man's whole day.

They took gratefully the little less he was prepared to give. Dani Larchmont had dared to ask for his heart—

She left the lane behind her, with its formidable wall of yews, and very soon found herself upon the main road to King's Beeches. Her long stripling's legs flashed whitely as she ran, and the rain, which the wind was driving straight into her face, flattened her hair into wringing wet tendrils on her forehead.

She didn't hear, right away, the sound of a galloping horse behind her, and the great, deep-chested roan was almost abreast of her before she did become aware. She flung round with a startled gasp, and when she saw who the rider was, she stared through the rain. His face was dark above her—he seemed to loom giant-like out of the rain, upon his great horse—riding her down. She tossed her dripping hair back from her face and pathetically she cried out: "It's only me—Rea! It's only me!"

"I know it's you, you funny drowned thing!" Burke laughed and the roan tossed its wild, proud head as he pulled him down to a trot and bent from the saddle to Rea. He held out his arms to her. "I won't leave you to be washed away," he said. "Come aboard." She hesitated, and then when she saw his fingers snap impatiently, she went into his arms. The muscles of his chest and his shoulders rippled beneath the tweed of his jacket as he lifted her into the saddle in front of him and he said to her: "You're not frightened of Rebel, are you?"

"No-no," she said.

"You seemed to be, just now."

"No, I'm all right."

"We startled you, eh?" Burke smiled, then he touched his spur to the roan and it leapt forward into a gallop.

CHAPTER NINE

ENCIRCLED by Burke's arm, with her head resting against his shoulder, Rea could watch his profile, and she found herself comparing the hard decisive chiselling of nose, mouth and chin, above which the Ryeland eyes shone as blindingly blue as perfectly matched sapphires and yet were never warm—like brilliant tropic seas that were ice-baths when plunged into, Rea thought—with the startling, decadent perfection of Jack Larchmont's face. A face that might have been stamped upon a Roman coin!

The thought was vaguely disturbing and Rea bit at her lip, remembering again the half bitter, half appealing look that face had worn when Jack had crouched at her knee and asked for her friendship.

Should she tell Burke she had met the Larchmonts?

The very next instant she forgot the Larchmonts, for Burke said to her: "I'm going up to London this weekend, Rea. The adoption people want me to sign Peter's final adoption papers." He smiled, his eyes travelling Rea's face, a rain-wet triangle against the grey-blue tweed of his jacket. "D'you want to come with me, pixie-face?" he asked. "After all, I did promise you a shopping spree, didn't I?"

"Did you?" She had forgotten, never deeply concerned with clothes and grown used to Iris Mallory's amusement that her wardrobe seemed so limited. But her heartbeats quickened at the mention of London. Oh, it would be nice to see London again. . . .

"You know I did, you unusual child." Burke amusedly flicked a raindrop, big as a pearl, from the tip of her left cheekbone. His finger felt the brittle fragility of the bone and stayed to trace the bone down to the side of her mouth. "I thought," he said, "we'd buy you something really staggering to wear to Iris's birthday dance. It's on Guy Fawkes' Night and she won't fail to invite us; she invariably invites the entire county."

"Oh, I'd love to come up to London!" Rea said quickly. "But what about Peter?—I don't really like the idea of leaving him."

Burke broke into indulgent laughter. "Oh, he'll be in good hands, Rea. Moira is the soul of duty and I rather fancy that with us out of the house Grandfather will find quite a lot of time to spend in the nursery."

"Then I will come!" But the smile that accompanied these words was hesitant, even a trifle shy. "Burke," she rubbed at the rough tweed of his jacket, "I don't want to come just to go shopping. I—I don't want you spending money on clothes for me. There's no need!"

"There's every need, you funny child, when it's something I want to do." Amusement, and a tinge of curiosity, were in his eyes as he watched her. "Don't you want to outshine the impeccable Iris?"

"Oh, Burke," her smile came and went, lifting the edges of her mouth, the pixie-line of her cheekbones, "I could never outshine Iris. She's far too handsome."

"Terribly, terribly handsome," Burke mocked. "The embodiment, in fact, of every county virtue in the book of county rules governing the selection of mates for all sons and daughters of ye olde county houses!" All at once his sapphire eyes were fairly dancing with sardonic amusement. "Rea, you funny, conscience-stricken baby, how much longer are you going to feel guilty about this marriage of ours? We've done fine, sweetheart. We've fooled everyone very satisfactorily."

"H-have we?" With a childish, burrowing movement, she hid her face in the rough warmth of his jacket. Its clinging scents of expensive cigarettes and horses tickled her nose and she rubbed the tickle away with the back of her hand. He didn't know, because she had never told him, that when he wasn't somewhere about King's Beeches, she became again its awkward intruder—its unwanted guest.

She had never told him about the hours she spent in quiet hiding. In deep window seats behind the fall of yards of thick curtaining. In little lonely arbours in the vast garden. Sometimes curled among the lower branches of the crowding apple trees in the orchard. He didn't know how acute an embarrassment it was for her when one of the many servants about the house had to come searching for her because there was a caller, and his grandfather, for propriety's sake, desired her to pour out tea and make polite conversation with the caller, who, nine times out of ten, as Rea well knew, had come to King's Beeches on purpose to examine herself. He didn't know that this realization so unnerved her that she poured more tea in the silver tray than in the teacups, and instead of making the polite conversation desired of her, she just sat gazing in tongue-tied misery at the bread and butter on her plate and blindly wishing she had never known Laura Damien and had therefore never had to go to Hastings. . . .

"I—I wish you had married Iris—anyone but me," she blurted out.

"Oh, don't you wish Iris on me," he protested.

"Your—your grandfather likes her. They laugh together when she comes to the house. She plays the piano to him. They—they understand one another. And I think, Burke," fiercely Rea rubbed at his jacket with her finger, making the rain-wet wool curl, "I think he'd have lost some of his bitterness towards you if you had married her."

"I've learned to accept, if not always tolerate, my grandfather's bitterness, Rea," Burke replied. "It's far more congenial to me than an over-fond, over-possessive wife would be."

"Don't you—don't you want to be loved?" Rea asked, in a rather strangled voice. "I mean—Iris—"

He was silent, and Rea pulled her face away from his jacket and looked up at him. Immediately he grinned, for she looked decidedly comical with one of her cheeks smudged red where she had pressed it to his jacket, and her fringe dripping raindrops into her eyes and making her blink. "Burke, what would you do if I became over-fond and over-possessive?" she demanded.

"You?" He laughed and gave her wet fringe an indulgent tweak. "I'd give you back to the 'little people.' "

It was rather a coincidence they should have been

talking about Iris Mallory, for she was at the house when Burke's roan trotted into the stable-yard.

She was in the armoury-room with Burke's grandfather, for he had taken her there to show her the curious Roman-type dagger one of his farm labourers had recently ploughed up. The armoury-room overlooked the stable-yard, and Iris stared hard out of the window as the roan's breath plumed into the cold air and Burke's rain-wet head gleamed black above the fair head of the girl in his arms. And they were laughing—laughing in the rain—the rain adding an intimacy to the scene that drove every particle of colour from Iris's face, leaving only the brilliant, staring green of her eyes.

"God, how I hate that girl—how I hate her!" she exclaimed.

Burke's grandfather glanced up from an absorbed examination of the dagger, which he considered every bit as fine as those in the Taunton Museum. He stared at Iris. Then he came to the window and gazed out with her upon the stable-yard, where Burke had just dismounted and was now lifting Rea from the back of the roan.

As he swung her to the kidney stones he said something that again made her chuckle, and old, hard, proud Mr. Ryeland, watching that small face crinkle and assume its pixie look, said somewhat dryly to Iris: "He's pixie-led, my dear. But better her, dammit, than that Larchmont girl!" He waved an expressive hand. "I couldn't have borne that. There's a wildness in that blood. Look at the boy; spends half his time in the Barley Mow, down at Shepton."

"She—died," Iris said, staring out at the wet stable-yard, suddenly emptied and quiet as Burke and Rea disappeared into the stable with the roan. He would rub the roan down himself, he always did, and Rea would watch, seated on an upturned box or a pile of saddles. The roan would steam horsily and the dull stable light would throw those delicate shadows under Rea's cheekbones. . . .

"Dani Larchmont died," Iris said again.

"Aye!" Old Mr. Ryeland nodded, curtly. "While he was in Peru she came here. Yes, she came *here*. Wanted me to give her his mailing address. I didn't have it, as a matter of fact, but I wasn't going to tell her that. I told her, instead, that he had left orders that I wasn't to divulge his mailing address to anyone. Humph," the hawk face wore a fleeting, rather grim smile, "she looked mighty queer when I said that—mighty queer. Ran from the house crying. It was obvious they'd had a row before he left for Peru."

Iris's long fingernails were digging into her palms as she listened, for here was one more cause for pain and hate—Dani Larchmont, that little farm-girl—

"Did you—did you see her again?" Iris demanded.

He shook his head. "No, and didn't want to! Then, as you know, those rumours about the loss of every member of that expedition Burke was with got into the papers. I met Jim Larchmont down in the village one morning and he stopped me to ask whether the rumours were true. As far as I knew, at that time, they were and I said so. The news couldn't have made very pleasant hearing for him. He'd have been mighty bucked, dammit, to have that witch-faced daughter of his married to a Ryeland and elevated to the county. But as far as we all knew, Burke was dead. And if it meant that he was thereby saved from the clutches of that gypsy creature, I wasn't sorry. I told Larchmont so."

"You—you actually said—that?" Iris's eyes flashed with angry shock. "Y-you wouldn't have cared if Burke had been dead—Burke?"

"My Philip was alive then," he returned flatly. "Burke never cared a dash about this place, All he wanted was to be off, over foreign hills, playing around. He was never a true Ryeland." The old face twisted with remembered hate; a bitterness that still persisted. "Writing books—mixing with creatures like that Larchmont girl! He ran around with her for years, and I cetainly wished him dead before I wished him married to her. I used to say to Philip, if that boy marries that offspring of those wild, queer Larchmonts, I'll forbid him this house while I live. I'll curse him up hill and down dale. I'll burn this house before he'll ever bring a son of hers into it. . . ."

Then the old man swallowed hard, waved his hand about as though he were momentarily lost for breath. "Ah, well, as things turned out, he wasn't to have her. He's got a son, but not from her, thank God!"

"But you know nothing of this—of this Rea he's brought here!" Iris flung out.

"I know what my eyes tell me." The thin shoulders, that wouldn't give in to age and stoop, lifted on a shrug. "She's a whey-faced fairy thing, I'll grant you that, but she's quietly enough bred. She's produced a fine lad in young Peter."

At this, Iris's jade-green eyes dilated to their fullest extent, flashing with pain and temper. "Don't throw that in my face!" she cried. "You tear me apart when you throw that in my face!"

"My dear—"

But she went on blindly: "For years, and you know it, I've lived with the hope that I might give Burke his sons. I—I'd lay down my life to do it! I love him—always—" She flung round with these words and leaned against the panelled wall beside the window, where rain beat quick, hard fingers against the leaded panes. Iris held her face in her hands, beyond pride, tortured by that picture of Rea in Burke's arms . . . tortured by the thought of that blue-eyed child upstairs. Always it seemed she had been wanting Burke Ryeland, and always it seemed he had been walking away from her, into other arms. . . .

Old Mr. Ryeland, with the jerky awkwardness of someone who is not naturally demonstrative, reached out and patted her shoulder. "It was my hope, too, my dear, all these months since Burke came back from Peru, that you and he should make a happy married life together. But it wasn't to be. He already had this girl. He was married—"

"He only married to give you what you wanted!" Iris retorted, her face showing for a moment through her hands, passionate, pale, but still very handsome. "He only married to secure the heirdom of King's

Beeches. He doesn't really care a penny-ha'penny about this girl. We both know it—and this—this plain little Jane—she sits in corners and pretends she isn't there. She make no demands upon him. She's quite content with the few crumbs of affection he throws her now and again, and it's evident he doesn't throw those very often. They've got separate rooms, haven't they? A whole corridor separates her from Burke. But I suppose, now he's got the baby—"

But old Mr. Ryeland, one of the old school, after all, wasn't prepared to discuss this intimate aspect of Burke's marriage; Burke's duty marriage.

"That's enough, Iris," he said curtly. "You're forgetting yourself."

"You mean I'm forgetting I'm a lady!" she flashed back. "I wish to God I wasn't! I should have been a little farm-girl, or a typist. Burke has quite a penchant for *them,* hasn't he?" Iris drew a sudden deep, shaking breath. "I could kill him, much as I . . . I could kill him and that stupid little typist, with her kid's fringe!"

"Iris," old Mr. Ryeland said, his fondness for her making him as gentle as he could be, "be a good girl, now. Grow up!"

"I'm grown up, thanks!" For a moment she confronted him with her hands on her shapely hips, then she swung disdainfully on her booted heel and left him.

Rea and Burke left for London early on Saturday morning.

Rea was excited. It showed in her eyes; an excitement that was half caused by the fact that she would be away from King's Beeches for a couple of days; away from the strain of acting and knowing she acted. Now she could be herself.

They arrived at Paddington Station around one o'clock and took a taxi to a hotel near Green Park.

As Burke signed the register, he and the clerk exchanged commonplaces in the manner of people who had met before, and it occurred to Rea that Burke had probably stopped here in the days when he had made all the continents his world of discovery and paid only duty visits to King's Beeches. The thought was vaguely worrying and she found, as they entered the lift, that she was studying his face for any sign that this quiet, very elegant hotel recalled to him those carefree, adventurous days. But his face was quite impassive. The blue eyes gave nothing away.

Rea had had a wash and was combing her hair in front of the dressing-table mirror in her room, when Burke lightly tapped upon the door that separated their rooms. "We won't have luncheon here at the hotel," he said, as he came across the room to her. "I know a delightful Spanish place in Piccadilly, quite near Madame Baum's, where, incidentally, I'm going to leave you for the afternoon, Rea."

"Madame Baum's?" Rea swung round on the dressing stool, her eyes opening wide in a quiet panic. "Is it—is it a dress shop?"

He nodded, taking hold of her hands and pulling her to her feet. "It's where Iris goes. And Iris, you will allow, is a very elegant dresser."

"But I'm not Iris's type!" Rea scuffed the coffee-and-cream carpet with the toe of her shoe. "She's terribly sophisticated. Why, I'd look awful—perfectly preposterous in the sort of clothes she can wear."

He laughed and marched her to the door. "Madame Baum won't put you into sequined sheaths and backless slipper satin, I promise you. She'll take one look at your funny pixie face and put you in Lincoln green and holly-berry red, not forgetting to attach a nodding cap with a bell on it to your head."

Madame Baum, in fact, put Rea into the kind of dresses Iris Mallory would have looked preposterous in. Rea had to admit herself that if she didn't assume dignity, she did assume a sort of ethereal Midsummer-Night quality .

The colours alone intrigued her.

One dress was all tangled pearl colours over an underskirt of rosy lilac. Another was a floating mist of cream merging into buttercup-yellow. Another was white with bunches of rich red cherries spread over it.

But Rea's favourite was in a light crimson, the shining silk of it suffused with gold. Little Madame Baum, with her quick, nasal voice and her plump, ring-laden hands, called it "Chrysanthemum."

Rea, gazing at herself in the tall fitting-room mirror and touching the rustling material with hands that shook slightly with nervous excitement, called it a magic dress. It did such amazing things to her appearance, adding a white luminosity to her skin, touching her hair to gold, and taking the childish solemnity out of her eyes and adding a womanly mystery she couldn't help noticing herself.

Her heart raced in her side.

This was the dress she would wear to Iris Mallory's birthday dance, and perhaps, for that one evening, people would not cast those curious, half speculative, half incredulous side-glances at Burke, as though they'd give anything to know whether actual choice or a reckless bottle of wine had prompted his marriage to such a naïve creature as herself.

There were other clothes as well, clothes which Rea hadn't even known she was to have, but it appeared that Burke had written to Madame Baum, informing her of their intended trip to London and giving her orders to supply his wife with a complete wardrobe, one that extended right down to bedroom slippers.

Rea was embarrassed. She tried not to show it, but the quick, worldly eyes of Madame Baum, who was so delighted by this extensive and unexpected order that she was ready to be delighted with Rea to the point of actual affection, saw her discomfiture and waved it away with her flashing fingers.

"Honey, I think you have a very fond husband," she said. "Be grateful—and let him spend his money." She broke into a laugh. "Think of his pleasure when he sees you in this." She held out an apricot slik nightdress for Rea's inspection and her dark eyes snapped with a delighted appreciation when Rea's cheeks bloomed red as summer peonies.

The bulk of Rea's new wardrobe was to be sent home to King's Beeches, but she knew Burke intended taking her out that evening, so she elected to take back to the hotel with her a little amber wool dress and a matching amber wool coat. Madame Baum fancied a little pillbox hat in black to go with the outfit, along with black suede shoes and black suede gloves. Rea complied with these smart fancies of Madame's, her eyes alight with young eagerness, her heart warm inside her with gratitude towards Burke. She had never possessed such clothes—had never thought to possess them!

Madame Baum came down in the lift with Rea, and as they crossed to the glistening maple doors, through which, during the course of the day, came actresses and elegant widows, debutantes and prospective brides, elderly wives and young wives, Madame reflected that rarely indeed did the quiet, self-effacing modesty of this girl come through her smart and famous doors. Her worldly heart was touched. The child's husband was rich and well-born (oh, yes, Madame had heard of King's Beeches!) yet there wasn't a spark of arrogance or complacency about her. The girl was genuinely nice; Madame had met too many of the other sort not to be able to see the difference. Such blushes as came to these young cheeks weren't forced there by determination and a too-tight girdle!

"Mrs. Ryeland," she paused, smiling, by the maple doors, "when you wear your so sweet little outfit tonight," she touched a ruby fingernail to the two ivory and salmon boxes Rea carried (Madame had wanted to send them to the hotel by a messenger, but Rea had said that she would be taking a taxi to the hotel and therefore saw no reason why she shouldn't take the boxes herself), "will you promise to wear the lipstick I have put in the little black bag? Just a little, just to make your lips glow. You will look so attractive." Madame's pert face, far from innocent of cosmetics, creased in a smile of lively encouragement. "Do it for your so generous husband. Promise, huh?"

Rea laughed, a trifle confusedly. "Madame Baum, you're encouraging me to be fast," she accused.

The ruby fingernail again tapped a tattoo upon the handsome dress boxes. "That you will never be, my child, and that makes your very generous husband a very lucky man."

Rea kept thinking of that remark as she rode back to the hotel.

It was perfectly natural, she supposed, for anyone as worldly as Madame Baum to accept beautiful dresses and shimmering lingerie as tokens of a rich man's affection. But as Rea regarded the ivory and salmon boxes upon her lap, a sudden little cloud of depression rode across the lightness of heart she had known all afternoon, trying on the beautiful dresses and handling lingerie that ran through her fingers like liquid silk. She loved the dresses—loved them—but it hurt a little that Burke would only want her to say an impersonal 'thank you' for his lovely gifts—for these gifts were not tokens of a husbandly affection, as Madame Baum supposed.

They were, these things, an extra guard against the suspicion that sometimes gleamed below the haughty scorn of Iris Mallory's green eyes.

And very possibly they also fed Burke's pride. He was a rich man, but for some weeks now Rea had reigned as his wife in a couple of cheap skirts, one belonging to her rust suit; some hand-knitted jumpers and her navy-blue dress. Now, however, Burke had provided her with a wardrobe that met royally all the demands of being his wife. Smooth tweed for when she took walks about the estate, tailored wool for when she took tea with those nerve-racking afternoon callers, real silk for sitting down to dinner in the dining-room that always seemed solemn with the weight of its exquisite candelabra, its Chelsea tureens, and its Venetian glass.

Rea stared at those ivory and salmon boxes from the House of Baum.

Real silk for Rea Glyn, who was now the wife of Burke Ryeland—in name only!

CHAPTER TEN

REA gazed in the mirror, half frightened by what she saw. She didn't hear Burke tap upon the door, didn't know he was in her room until he loomed up in the mirror behind her. She stood very still, her slender figure, in the swoothly woven amber wool, tensing as Burke's hands came to her shoulders and he slowly turned her towards him.

Then, with a nervous little rush, Rea said: "It's a nice dress, isn't it? They're all so nice, my new dresses!" With shy gratitude she rubbed her cheek against one of his hands. "I'm so grateful, Burke, I could cry."

"Don't you dare!" He gave her a tiny shake. "Tears and sophisticated amber wool don't go together."

"It isn't sophisticated, is it?" She glanced down at herself. "I don't look silly or anything, do I?"

"Take another look in that mirror," he commanded. "Now tell me what you see."

She looked in the mirror, but not at herself. She smiled at Burke, tall and distinguished in an impeccable dark suit. "How awesome you look," she murmured.

"I'm not awesome." He trailed light fingers across her cheek, quizzing the soft red glow of her lightly lipsticked mouth with amused eyes. "For once, my dear, I'm as nice and mild as Cheddar cheese." He swung round, saw her new coat lying across the foot of the bed and picked it up. He helped her into it, carefully straightening its full, dashing folds.

"I've a hat, as well." She darted across to the tallboy and collected the little black pillbox. "It hasn't got a bell on it, though. Are you sorry?"

His brown cheeks creased as he leant against the dressing-table and watched her adjust the jaunty little hat upon her head. She looked charming, he thought. A charming child, playing at being grown up!

"Do you like yourself now, Rea?" he enquired.

She smiled. "I don't think I am myself," she said. "I feel as though—as though I've been taken over, like someone in an H. G. Wells story. I think I shall wake up presently and find myself back on Hastings pier, watching the lights dancing on the water like a cascade of diamonds."

"Will this help to strengthen the spell or break it?" Burke withdrew his hand from his pocket and came to her. He took hold of her right hand and fitted on to her wrist a delightful little lozenge-shaped watch, attached to a wisp of a gold strap. "Like it?" he murmured.

"Oh, Burke! Oh, I can't take it!" She stared at the little watch. "You've given me so much already—too much!"

"Tokens of very sincere appreciation, believe me, Rea." He held up her hand, admiring the delicate partnership of slender, blue-veined wrist and tiny gold watch. "You did more than come to King's Beeches to take up an invidious position, you took little Peter into your heart. And that love of yours for Peter has secured his position at King's Beeches far more effectively than my individual affection for him would have done." Burke smiled. "Are you aware that Grandfather is most impressed by your devotion to your young son?"

"Has he—has he said so," Rea's eyes were wide with amazement.

Burke, still smiling, hugged her gently. "Yes, my dear, he has actually said so. Now hurry up and get into your best coat, we're going out to the lushest restaurant I can find."

And it was lush!—decorated in silver and turquoise, with chandeliers that were like glistening fairy castles set in a domed roof of translucent turquoise glass, with a band whose music was like smooth cream, Rea thought, and a waiter who had the dignity of a bishop.

He reverently brought and placed their apricot jam omelettes and Rea gazed after him in undisguised delight. "He's lovely!" she said to Burke. "He reminds me of Tolliver."

"The estimable Tolliver, my child, wouldn't appreciate being likened to a waiter," Burke retorted. "Tolliver has been called the most perfect butler in Somerset."

"He's very fond of Peter, you know." Rea delicately licked delicious apricot jam from the side of her mouth. "He takes him out in the pram. And do you know," her eyes laughed across the table into Burke's, "he still looks as dignified as Cromwell. I like him. He doesn't make me feel in the least an—an intruder."

"Well, you're not an intruder, you're the mistress of King's Beeches."

"No!" She shook her head in quick negation, her smile darting out of sight and a sudden wash of embarrassed pink in her cheeks. She hated to be called—that! Intruder was the right word; Burke couldn't gild it into "mistress" with a pleasant smile and a wardrobe of expensive clothes. "Burke, don't let us pretend when we're alone," she begged.

"I'm not pretending, you silly little thing!" His eyes laughed at her as he dabbed at his lips with a table napkin. "I know you've got a secret yen to see me landed with Iris Mallory, but Iris eats her men—skin, bones—feet!"

"Oh—you!" Rea had to laugh.

"Did you pick out a perfectly fabulous dress to wear at Iris's party?" Burke asked.

She nodded. "But I'm going to keep it shut away until the night of the party. I'm not even going to show it to you."

"How unkind! I've a good mind not to give you a second glass of champagne."

He squeezed her hand—and then lost all laughter as he caught sight of someone beyond her left shoulder. The woman was rapidly bearing down upon them, swathed in a cerise dress that did battle with the rouge upon her cheeks, her eyes almost bolting from her head. Burke was wincing long before she exclaimed, at Rea's elbow: "Well, I never did! If it isn't little Rea Glyn!"

Rea's head jerked round towards the speaker and her soft mouth made an O of unutterable dismay as she found herself staring straight into the hard blue eyes of Laura Damien—eyes that were distended to their fullest extent, avid with curiosity.

Then Burke drawled: "Won't you join my wife and me in a glass of wine, Mrs. Damien?" He released Rea's hand, rose to his feet and politely pulled out a chair for Laura—and he and she stared at one another as she took the proffered chair. She was pink and hot and bursting with questions; he was cool and sardonic and fully prepared, Rea could see, to enjoy Laura's questions.

"So it was you!" she burst out.

"It was I." He poured champagne, then lounged back in his chair, sipping the shimmering liquid with imperturbable appreciation.

"You might have told me!" Laura flung across the table at Rea. "It's hardly believable! How long have you been married?"

"We knew one another exactly a fortnight," Burke drawled. "Romantic, eh?"

Laura gave a harsh laugh. "You're a cool one, Burke," she said. "It was you, I suppose, who told Rea not to tell me. Why the secrecy?"

"Because I like cheese with my apple pie."

"You knew I'd ask questions," Laura shot back at him. "You knew I'd be very interested to know why you—you of all people," the finger she shook at him was waggish, "should want to marry my little Rea. After all, my dear, neither of us can pretend that she sparkles, exactly. A good, sweet child—but—" She laughed at him over the rim of her wine glass and her laugh plainly said: "But we both know that a man of the world—your kind of world—wants more than that."

"A good, sweet child," Burke echoed. He grinned wickedly at Laura. "Aren't I the lucky one?"

"She told me she was going into the country to look after a little boy." Laura gave a rather coarse guffaw. "Did you tell her to say that?"

"As a matter of fact, I didn't," he replied. "How clever of her!"

"Oh, I'll admit she's been clever," Laura retorted significantly. She took another gulp at her champagne, then she said brashly: "She's a damn good typist, but I can't see her ladying it over that regiment of servants you must have at King's Beeches. D'you know," Laura's laughter was huskily malicious, "she used to fall over her own tongue giving orders to a hotel bell-boy."

Her bold blue eyes swung to Rea. "Didn't you, my dear?"

"D-did I?" Rea flushed to her fringe, for how well that malicious remark of Laura's described the kind of person she had been—still was, despite the expensive dress she wore tonight.

Shy and stupid, Laura's remark said, and Rea slowly lowered her eyes to the champagne glass in her hand, her joy in her smart little dress, this glamorous restaurant, the charming nonsense Burke had been talking only a matter of minutes ago dying out of her, leaving her chilled and depressed. She was just a dressed-up puppet —and Laura Damien seemed to know it.

"Did I?" she said again. Then she lifted her head and her eyes fully confronted Laura's. On a rising note of defiance, she added: "Wasn't I stupid? But then I am rather stupid. I still 'stupidly blush,' as you used to call it."

"Ooh, temper!" Laura laughed, opening her eyes up wide.

But Burke didn't laugh, though Laura half looked at him, as though expecting him to.

All at once he seemed to lose his amusement at the situation. Abruptly he jerked back his chair and rose to his feet. "Sorry to break up the party, Mrs. Damien," he said, "but Rea and I have tickets for Covent Garden. We'll be late if we don't get a move on." He strode round the table and almost lifted Rea out of her chair. Brusquely he helped her on with her coat.

"So you still go to the ballet?" Laura drawled, also rising and negligently shaking out the rustling skirt of her cerise dress. "It was always a weakness of yours, wasn't it, my dear? I've never forgotten the utterly lovely face of that little ballet-dancer you used to be so friendly with. What became of her? Did she retire from dancing?"

Rea, listening, drew in her breath, for Burke's hands about her arms had become bands of iron, torturing her flesh, though he seemed entirely unaware of the fact. He held her against his breast, staring over her head at Laura Damien. "She died," he said, curtly.

"Why, the poor child!" Laura's eyes opened wide, their painted lashes standing out stiffly all round those staring blue globes. "So young, so talented—so lovely! Oh, you poor boy, what a tragic loss for you—you could never, never replace her!" Her eyes left Burke and raked Rea's face. "You had to see that little girl, Rea, to appreciate the absolute loveliness of her. She was so happy and sweet, too! Always laughing, she was. So *alive*, so full of sparkle." She glanced back at Burke, having got this thrust in at Rea, who seemed to shrink into even smaller and paler proportions against Burke as she, too, remembered the enchanting face of that dead girl. "Burke," Laura demanded, "whatever did she die of? I mean, my dear, she was so young."

"She was twenty-seven," he returned. "She probably overworked. The life of a ballet-dancer isn't an easy one, you know."

"Of course not." Laura held a square of cerise chiffon to her chin, her glance archly sympathetic as it travelled Burke's dark, unsmiling face and finally settled on Rea, held like a small shield against his broad chest. "Do you know, I still can't quite take it in. You and little Rea—married!" she burst out.

"If I had my marriage lines on me, Mrs. Damien, I'd exhibit them just to ease your mind," Burke returned, with deliberate rudeness.

"Oh, I didn't mean—" she laughed, waving the square of chiffon about in the air, actually a trifle embarrassed. "I meant, dear boy, that it's such a surprising match, you and little Rea. She's such a shy, retiring child." Then, as Burke refrained from answering, merely returning her stare of bold curiosity with a blank impassiveness, she gave another laugh and glanced across the room, to where somebody waved impatiently from a table close to the circular dais where the band played. "I must go," she said. "My friends across the way are getting impatient. It has been fun, meeting again."

"If you say so, Mrs. Damien," Burke drawled.

Laura laughed as her glance settled again on Rea. "You'll have to invite me down to King's Beeches, my dear," she insinuated, a coy quirk to her large, painted mouth. "I'd adore to see the place."

"But, Mrs. Damien," Burke said, lifting an eyebrow at her, "we're still in the throes of our honeymoon. We'd be very dull company for you. We hold hands all day long."

"Do you?—how sweet!" Laura's smile, however, wasn't very sweet as she watched the sudden little flags of colour flying on the delicate thrusting of Rea's cheekbones. She might well blush, Laura thought. Deep little chit!

"Oh, well," Laura said, "invite me later, dear boy. We'll talk about the old days."

"The old days?" Burke stared at her and once again his hands closed bruisingly upon Rea's slender arms. "They're part of a book I don't read any more, Mrs. Damien."

"Because of that poor lovely girl!" Laura tut-tutted sympathetically. "I see—oh, I do see! The things you have don't really compensate—do they?" Once again she waved her handkerchief about. Then she exclaimed: "Oh dear, my friends are making frantic signals again—that's my publisher, sitting beside the long-necked creature in green! I really must go, my dears! So lovely, meeting again!"

She was gone with the words, threading her large, cerise-enshrouded figure between the tables, leaving behind her a wave of silence and perfume. Burke slowly, slowly relaxed his hold upon Rea's arms. "So hellish, meeting again!" he amended.

Rea lay staring into the darkness. She had, she discovered, grown so used to the majestic and feathery comfort of her four-poster at King's Beeches, that this stream-lined hotel bed seemed strangely small and comfortless in comparison. She turned first this way, then that, telling herself it was the bed that was keeping her awake.

But it wasn't the bed alone.

Her mind was dancing with faces and thoughts and the remembrance of things said throughout this strange, long day. The luxurious scent of Madame Baum's dress shop still seemed to linger in her nostrils; the rasping surprise of Laura Damien's voice to linger in her ears; the fluttering, glittering birds of the Covent Garden stage to go on leaping and spinning before her eyes.

Oh, she couldn't stand it, this restless floating upon a wave of scent and colour and voices! She sat up, reaching out a hand and snapping on the bedside lamp. If only she had a book—anything to quieten her mind, strung to such a discordant pitch, like an over-wound violin. She glanced round the elegant hotel bedroom, but there were no books, no magazines. She sighed and clasped her arms about her updrawn knees.

How awful it had been, running into Laura Damien again! It had spoiled the whole evening. Burke had turned so moody and taciturn, and throughout the ballet Rea had seemed to see Dani Larchmont. Every whirling bird was Dani. Every vivid face upon that stage belonged to her. Every slender leg and beckoning arm . . .

Burke had made no comment on the ballet as they had left, and his taciturn manner had all too successfully reawakened a tongue-tied shyness in Rea. She had sat small and mouse-quiet in the taxi that bore them back to their hotel, the smoke of Burke's cigarette drifting to her, stinging her constricted throat. She felt, suddenly, that her presence, in the taxi and in his life, was resented by him—and why not! If Laura Damien's reappearance into their lives had reawakened his memories of Dani Larchmont, then he must resent her presence. Her good, sweet, childish presence!

Rea's small teeth restlessly nibbled her bottom lip; nibbled and nibbled, till the lip burned. Poor Burke, saying to her, Rea: "Does one ever stop paying for one's mistakes?" Wanting Dani—wanting and wanting—now it was too late. Rea's arms tightened about her knees. Somehow she would have liked to have brought him a little comfort—

Then her head jerked up and she stared at her door, for it had opened and Burke stood tall in the wide-thrown aperture of it. "I woke up—and saw your light under the door." He tied the silk cord of his dressing-gown and crossed the room to her. "Are you all right?"

"I couldn't sleep." She hesitated to give him a smile,

he looked so dark, so almost grim, in the dark silk of his dressing-gown. "I'm sorry my light woke you."

"No," he waved her apology away, "it wasn't your light. I was restless before I fell asleep." He sat down on the side of her bed, running a tidying hand over his sleep-ruffled hair. "Why can't you sleep?" he asked.

"Oh," she gave a little shrug, "I think I'm missing Peter. I always bath him for Moira, you know, and I keep wondering if he's missed me. He looks so adorable, straight out of his bath." Her face grew wistful as she thought of the warm, wriggling, shrimp-pink baby upon her towel-draped lap, his blue eyes sparkling up at her as she played "this little piggy went to market" with his toes.

With a motion that was curiously lost and seeking, Rea laid her face against her knees. "Is Peter at all like his mother?" she murmured.

Burke shook his head. "No. He has my brother Phil's nose and mouth, and luckily for me, those Ryeland eyes."

"Her eyes were dark, weren't they — dark as a gipsy's?"

"Yes, but how did you know?" A sudden frown drew down Burke's eyebrows as he watched Rea's face, turned sideways to him upon her knees.

"I've seen her portrait. While I was out walking — that afternoon it rained and you took me home on Rebel—I met Mr. Larchmont and he invited me into his farmhouse to meet Mrs. Larchmont. I saw the portrait in her room." Rea's eyes met Burke's and they smiled gently. "I can quite understand why you love her as you do."

"Because you've seen her portrait and think her beautiful?" he returned curtly.

"Yes." Rea nodded. "She must have been so full of life. I could almost hear her laughter."

"Yes—she laughed a lot." Abruptly he rose from the bed and began to prowl about the room, idly lifting Rea's small black gloves and dropping them back on the dressing-table, flicking at the pink fringe of the bedside lamp. "Rea, my grandfather mustn't ever learn that Peter is half a Larchmont. He dislikes the family intensely. Dani, I'm afraid, was another of his many counts against myself." Burke shrugged. "He thought I wanted to marry her."

"Didn't you?" Rea spoke gently.

"I never wanted to marry anyone! That was the trouble—the beginning and the end of it—if we've seen the end of it!" He regarded Rea with moody eyes. "I've always taken, Rea. Always taken. Being born a Ryeland placed too many advantages in my lap at too early an age; they made me selfish! I took and wasn't prepared to give back, as Phil was. I wanted freedom and scope and the world to toss like a shining ball—and I tossed it. I wanted the laughter and the gaiety of a girl like Dani, but once again I wasn't prepared to give back. Let her amuse me! Let her dance to the tunes I piped! Lord," he drew a deep, harsh breath, "when I look back—when I think of my own arrogance! Dani would be alive now if she had never known me!"

"Oh, no!" Rea shook her head in quick protestation, sitting up straight in her bed. "You mustn't believe that, Burke. It isn't true."

"You're a fatalist, eh?" He looked cynical. "You believe that a Higher Authority writes finis to our earthly adventure, eh?"

Her fingers plucked at the sheets upon her bed. "I—think I believe that."

"Because it softens the blow, Rea!" he retorted. "Because it makes things less terrible, less bleak, to be able to say to oneself: 'This person I'm fond of has died because his, or her, allotted moment to die has come.' Well, I can't think like that, Rea. I can't say it."

"Then your heart will never stop aching, Burke. Your heart will always wear its bruise."

"I know." He gave a harsh laugh. "It's aching now, my heart." Abruptly he came to the side of her bed and stood staring down at her. "How young you look," he said.

"Do I?" She gazed up at him. "Yet I'm nineteen. I'm not a child."

"You're a mere baby—and I've made you look sad. Damn my black heart, you're to stop thinking about it!"

He bent to her and took her face in his hands. "I want you to be happy," he said simply.

"I am happy, when I'm with you and Peter." She smiled a quick smile.

"Rea, you're to promise me you'll keep away from the Larchmont farm." Burke's hands tipped her face, so that her eyes met his, fully. "It's a melancholy place."

"And your grandfather would be annoyed if he knew I went there!" Rea finished for him. "Oh, it seems such a shame! Mrs. Larchmont sees so few people. And I felt so sorry for her."

"All the same, keep away from the place, Rea." He went to straighten up, but suddenly Rea's arms were about his neck. "Burke," she said, "you're so good to me and I'm terribly grateful. So grateful for all those lovely clothes—and the little watch." And quickly, rather confusedly, as though she feared he would repulse her, she brushed her lips across his cheek.

She felt him tense, felt his jaw harden even before she drew her lips away. She shrank against her pillows, feeling as though she had poached. "Why—why do you look like that?" she stammered. "A-are you angry?"

"This is rather a dangerous time of the night—or morning, rather—for kisses." Now he was looking sardonic as he carefully removed her arms from around his neck. "I'm pleased you like the dresses and the watch, Rea. Now you must go to sleep, like a good child." He watched her slide down in the bed and cover herself to the chin. Then he snapped off the bedside lamp and left her.

Still she didn't sleep immediately.

The night closed round her in stillness, and in a little while there stole into her room, from the room next door, the scent of a cigarette; and it suddenly seemed to Rea that she had never known anything more lonely than the drifting scent of Burke's cigarette, coming to her through the darkness and the silence.

She sighed and turned her face upon her arm, and even as she grieved for Burke's loneliness, she resolved that never again would she thrust her unwanted kisses upon him.

Her face burned against the linen of her pyjama sleeve and she slid down even farther in her bed. Burke had thought—oh, she knew what he had thought! But she hadn't intended a beguilement with that kiss. Beguile Burke—whose heart ached this night for the lovely, tragic Dani Larchmont?

CHAPTER ELEVEN

TOLLIVER had barely got the front door open before Rea was racing past him with a breathless: "Hullo, Tolliver! It's lovely to be home—I must go up to Peter!" leaving Burke and the butler to gaze after her in a shared, spontaneous amusement. She wore the little rust suit in which Burke had proposed to her and it made her look almost ridiculously like a rusty, long-legged young greyhound as she sped the length of the hall and then went running up the stairs, her face alight with eager impatience.

Rea threw open the door of Peter's nursery — and came to an abrupt standstill, just inside the door. The greeting she had ready for Moira died on her lips, for Moira wasn't in the nursery.

Iris Mallory, very chic in filmy black chiffon, was sitting in the window seat, holding Peter in her arms and laughing up at Tab Gresham. Old Mr. Ryeland sat rather grimly on the edge of Moira's rocking-chair, the formality of his dark evening clothes, his silver hair and his mouth that grew thin as he saw Rea, making him very out of place among the frivolous chintz coverings of the chair.

The immediate resentment that flared in Rea at sight of Iris Mallory holding Peter—her Peter—took second place to concern as her eyes settled on Tab Gresham. "Why are you here, Tab—Peter isn't ill, is he?" She darted across the room with all the possessive anxiety of a true mother and went to take hold of Peter. But Iris deliberately tightened her arms about him, laughing up maliciously into Rea's concerned young face. "So the prodigal mother returns," she drawled.

"Peter's quite all right, Mrs. Ryeland," Tab Gresham reassured her, smiling at her. "I've been invited over to dinner, that's all."

"Oh!" Rea's face relaxed. "I thought, seeing you, that Peter's sore throat had come back." She bent over the baby, touching his cheek. "Hullo, Peter boy! Have you missed me?"

"You better had, old chap," Burke laughed, strolling into the room. "Your young mother has missed you." He glanced round at the company, his eyebrows quirking. "I say, is the gathering in honour of our return?"

His grandfather snorted, while Iris said: "How was London, my dear? Did you enjoy your break from rural duties—when your young wife wasn't pining for her son?"

"Oh, I saw to it that she didn't pine the entire weekend," Burke quipped, coming straight across the nursery to Iris and lifting the baby out of her arms. He swung him high, his dark face breaking into a boyish smile. "Hullo, youngster!" he cried, and was quite unconscious of the brilliant dilation of Iris's green eyes as they rested upon him. He looked particularly attractive and vigorous this evening in expensively tailored light grey, and he and the chuckling, handsome baby made quite a pair.

Iris felt her heart come into her throat. She loved him so! It wasn't fair—in fact it was ludicrous that this man should belong to—to this little typist—this schoolgirl! Iris's hating glance swept Rea from head to foot. That suit! It was priceless. Couldn't Burke see what a sight she looked? Didn't he care enough even to notice?

Then Burke said: "I say, Rea, you can just see Pete's two new teeth when he laughs."

"Can you really?" Rea eagerly took hold of Peter's dumpling fists as Burke lowered him towards her. "Laugh at me, darling," she begged of the baby, and when he good-naturedly obliged and she glimpsed those two minute teeth, she looked as awestruck as though she had suddenly struck gold. "Why, they're like little seedpearls!" she gasped.

She glanced round at Tab Gresham. "Have you seen Peter's teeth, Dr. Gresham?" she asked.

"Yes—dear—we've all seen them," Iris drawled. She rose gracefully to her feet and took hold of Mr. Ryeland's arm. "Shall we go downstairs?" she asked, looking bored. "You can play to me."

"Didn't you want to see the baby bathed?" he asked.

"Hardly, darling!" she retorted, and with that they went from the room. As the door closed on them, Tab

Gresham exclaimed: "I'd like to take a slipper to that girl!"

"Why don't you?" Burke laughed, lowering himself into the chintz of the rocking-chair his grandfather had just vacated and dancing Peter upon his knee. "She might come to her senses, then, and decide to fall in love with you. It's what you want, isn't it?"

Tab flushed slightly. "She'll never look my way," he said. "And even if she did, I could never give her the kind of life she's been used to."

"No?" Burke looked amused as he gently touched the dimple in Peter's chin. "She'd take you by the scruff of your neck and plonk you down in Harley Street. At the end of six months you'd be the most sought-after and fashionable physician in the whole area."

"I'd rather go without Iris than be that!" Tab retorted.

The two men stayed with Rea to see Peter bathed, then they went downstairs. She was rather wet—Peter, taking his bath, resembled a frolicsome puppy taking a swim; arms and legs were much employed in the operation and as a result water was inclined to fly in all directions—and had to go along to her room to change her dress. She had opened the wardrobe and was just about to lift out her navy-blue linen, when she thought of the little amber wool dress. She spun around on her heel and saw that the box it was in had been brought up from downstairs. She swooped on the box and eagerly lifted off the lid. Tonight she need not look dowdy beside Iris in her smart chiffon. Tonight she could wear a dress that was charming, expensive and becoming.

Yes, it was becoming, she decided, smoothing the wool down over her hips and gazing at herself in one of the long mirrors set in the doors of the wardrobe. It fitted beautifully. She looked neither a boy nor a schoolgirl in it. A happy little smile was playing about her lips as she energetically applied a brush to her hair. Then, neat and gleaming, she hurried from the room and made her way downstairs.

She could hear the sound of the piano before she reached the drawing-room, but she knew, as her fingers touched the handle of the door, that it wasn't Iris who was playing. She slipped into the room, her eyes opening wide with surprise when she saw Mr. Ryeland at the piano. And he played, she thought, much better than Iris.

She sank quietly into one of the chairs, suppressing a quick little smile as she saw Iris slowly scrutinize her from head to foot, a flash of disagreeable surprise plain in her eyes. She was sharing a couch with Burke, who lay back in a cat-like ease, a cigarette between his lips and his blue eyes half shut as he watched his grandfather.

Tab Gresham came behind Rea's chair and bent to murmur in her ear: "We're drinking sherry, Mrs. Ryeland. Shall I pour you one?"

"I'd prefer cider," she whispered, and as he went to move over to the sideboard, she caught at his sleeve. "And do call me Rea."

"If you'll promise to retaliate and call me Tab," he whispered back. "A nonsensical name, I know, but it's short for Talbot."

"I'll retaliate," she promised, and watched him go to the sideboard to pour her drink. It had surprised her to learn that he harboured an affection for Iris. He seemed too sensible, too solid, to fall in love with the glamour Iris represented in both a physical and a social sense. He seemed the type who would either remain a bachelor or marry a solid, dependable girl, one who would reap every fraction of worth and joy out of being a country doctor's wife. Besides, Iris was in love with Burke. It showed in every glance she gave him. It showed now in the very way she was sitting beside him, her left hand lightly brushing his shoulder, her eyes watching his profile, her mouth lushly red, lushly inviting in her smoothly tanned face. Rea was amazed, even a little shocked, that Iris should show her love so openly. A pagan love, Rea thought; uninhibited, unashamed, and still Burke's to take if he wished, despite the wife and child he had brought home to King's Beeches.

Tab brought Rea's glass of cider to her and settled himself in a chair at her side.

"Are you musical?" he asked.

"I like music and I can play the piano—a little. I play by ear, though."

"Is that bad?" Tab grinned. "I mean, aren't you supposed to?"

She smiled and shook her head.

After they had eaten dinner and returned to the drawing-room, Iris suggested some bridge. "There's four of us," she said.

"There's five of us," Tab Gresham put in quietly.

"Oh, I don't play," Rea said quickly. "You people go right ahead. I'll be perfectly happy just watching."

"Are you sure, Rea?" Burke watched her across the flame of a match as he lit a cigarette. Then he shook out the match and tossed it into the fire. "It isn't an exciting occupation, watching other people play cards."

"Don't you sew, dear, or knit?" Iris queried, her tone implying that if Rea was capable of doing anything, sewing and knitting possibly represented the sum total of her abilities.

"I read." Rea jumped to her feet. "I won't disturb you people at all. I'll take a cider and go to the library and read. I expect there's still a fire."

"Bring your book in here," Burke said.

"No, you'll disturb me." She smiled quickly at him, poured herself some cider from the small cask on the sideboard and slipped quietly away.

About half an hour later, quite unexpectedly, the door of the library opened and then closed, and when Rea looked round the side of the big library couch, where she was curled among some big green velvet cushions with a book in her lap, her enquiring eyes met the grey-blue eyes of Tab Gresham. "The brainy ones have thrown me out on my ear," he said, coming to the couch. "They are now playing three-handed something or other. I'm going to talk to you—I've been dying to ever since I sat down to play my tortuous bridge."

"What a gallant speech, Dr.—I mean Tab," she smiled.

"May I join you?" he came round the couch and sat down beside her. "May I also say that I like your dress, Rea? It's a beautiful colour."

"Yes, it is nice, isn't it?" She took a fold of the amber wool in her fingers, admiring it. "Burke has bought me the most wonderful wardrobe of clothes. I've never had such lovely things!" Her eyes shone into Tab's as she showed him her wrist, bearing Burke's little watch. "He gave me this, too. Isn't it lovely?"

"Very lovely," he took her wrist in his hand, but his eyes were upon her face. "Tell me, Rea, you don't worry about Iris at all, do you? I mean," Tab's forehead corrugated in a frown, "you may have noticed that she doesn't bother to hide—what she feels for Burke. She hoped to marry him, you know, and she's the sort who doesn't let go of the things she wants very easily. What I want to say is, don't let her attitude bother you. She couldn't coax Burke into her web while he was single, so she'll not succeed now that he's married—and very happily married, might I add."

"Do you really think that?" Rea searched Tab's face with her large eyes, pushing at her fringe as she always did when perplexed. "I wish—I wish I could make him happy."

"But you have!" Tab looked down at her in surprise. "You've given him yourself—and Peter."

"Y-yes, of course." Rea glanced away from Tab's half smiling blue-grey eyes in some confusion. "We may not be enough, though. I think he still longs to travel. It seems hard that he should be tied here at King's Beeches when his heart yearns for far places—don't you think?"

"No, I don't, as a matter of fact." Tab spoke with quiet decision. "In my opinion, happy domesticity is the best thing any man can have. Perhaps that sounds funny, coming from a stick-in-the-mud bachelor like myself, but I'll warrant Burke is settling down as a family man much better than you may think. Look at him tonight with Peter!"

"Yes, he loves Peter," she agreed, but still she kept her eyes turned from Tab's and he watched her in a growing puzzlement. It was funny, he thought, the way she seemed to grow a shell and to creep in under its protection whenever the talk veered round to her marriage. She seemed—she seemed almost frightened of talking about her marriage.

Tab's perplexed glance drew away from Rea's averted profile and settled on the low red glimmering of the fallen logs in the fireplace. There was, it had to be admitted, a decided mystery attaching to Burke's meeting and marriage with this young, sweet, unworldly girl. Tab couldn't believe, somehow, that she had ever been anywhere near Peru. He felt, in fact, that she had never been out of England in her life.

Yet if that were true—if that were true, where had they met, and when?

It was very definite that Burke had been in Peru. It had been the very devil trying to get into contact with him at the time of Philip's death. His expedition had been scattered, some of the members dead, and it had been some months before Burke had rejoined civilization and learned of his brother's death. He had come home immediately, but he had not mentioned a wife and child —the wife and child he must have had at that time.

Tab's sandy brows drew together in a frown. What was it Burke's grandfather was always saying? "Peter's like my Philip. The little lad is my Philip all over again." Tab felt his nerves give the same sort of jolt they might have given had he suddenly touched a faulty electric light switch and received a shock. Lord, what was he thinking? The child was Burke's—Burke's and this little girl's. One only had to see them with the child to realize they worshipped him.

Tab threw off his puzzling thoughts and returned his glance to Rea, a small golden and white figure among her huge green cushions. She had kicked off her shoes and Tab's sandy brows quirked amusedly at the doll-like proportions of her feet. Iris might call this girl a colourless little ninny, but Iris was a woman, she wouldn't see in Rea what a man—a man of sensitivity—would see. Rea might be laid out in pastels, Tab thought, but her colours would never fade, nor her value depreciate.

"I suppose," he said, "you'll be going to Iris's birthday dance next week?"

"If she invites me." Rea grinned. "Does she invite wives to her birthday dances?"

"Rather! She uses them for fuel on the big bonfire they always have in the forecourt of the house. The dance falls on Guy Fawkes' Night, you know."

"Yes, so Burke told me."

"Will you save me some dances, Rea?" He looked coaxing. "Nine times out of ten I arrive late and can't find a sausage to dance with."

"A sausage?" She chuckled. "I'm more like one of those skinny things they sell in delicatessen shops. But I'd love to dance with you, Tab—if I can manage to persuade Iris not to shovel me on to her bonfire." Relaxed and easy again, now that Tab had ceased to talk about her marriage, Rea laid her head back against the couch and the slight shifting of her body sent the book on her lap slithering to the floor. Tab bent to retrieve it, his eys on the title. "Ah, another book of Burke's, I see?" he exclaimed. He opened the book at the dedication page. "I remember him writing this, Rea. He'd never done a novel before. Are you enjoying it?"

Rea considered, watching Tab as he scanned the dedication, which was a single line from a poem of John Keats'; 'Two witch's eyes above a cherub's mouth.' A dedication that was not obscure to Rea, for she had seen Dani Larchmont's portrait. Then she said: "The book's beautifully written, of course, but it makes me sad."

Tab smiled slightly. "Burke sees dreams like pennies, Rea, with a reverse side, and here he was fascinated by the reverse side. You don't like it, eh, that Paul is never going to have his Caprice?"

Rea smiled and shook her head. "You're giving me an awfully male look, Tab. I suppose you think women soft, wanting dreams to come true all the time?"

"No, Rea." He smiled as he closed Burke's novel. "Men, even doctors, sometimes want their dreams to come true. We're all vulnerable in that direction. If we couldn't hope that tomorrow, or the day after, the something we want is going to be ours, life would become very dry in the mouth—" then he broke off and glanced up from Rea's absorbed young face, for the door had opened. The next moment Tab's eyes smiled in a rather cynical fashion, as if to say: "We won't talk of dreams any more, Rea. Those dreams are our secrets." And Rea understood, for there was a click of very high heels as Iris walked into the room.

She burst out laughing as she came to the couch and leant over the back of it. "Ooh, la la, this is cosy!" She turned and beckoned to Burke, who came across the room with long, lazy strides. "Get these two, my dear. Curled up together as cosy as you please." Her jade eyes mockingly roved Rea's face. "So this is why you've never learnt to play cards, dear?"

"Yes, isn't she clever?" Tab murmured, his face once again the composed face of the professional man as he watched Iris, above himself and Rea.

Burke strolled past the couch to the fireplace, amusedly lifting his eyebrows at the cosy picture Rea and Tab did make as they sat amidst the big green cushions. "What absurd little feet you've got, Rea," he remarked, in passing.

Rea immediately bent over double, fumbling on the floor for her shoes. That voice! That "uncle" voice, which he used upstairs in the nursery when he talked to Peter, and which he would use to *her,* in front of Iris. He knew it amused Iris. "My absurd feet go with the absurd rest of me," she retorted, her cheeks burning both from her annoyance and the difficulty she was having in locating her right shoe, which was half way under the couch.

Iris, watching her, gave a trill of laughter. Then she said to Burke: "Do you think she's absurd, my dear—all over?"

"Of course she is." Burke's blue eyes had lit up with a sudden mischief, ignited from Rea's unusual display of temper, and also from something touchingly young and lost about her that the fashionable dress intensified rather than took away. He stepped to the couch and with one lithe movement lifted Rea, holding her against his chest. "She's as absurd as Peter's pink elephant, aren't you?" His blue eyes came down to Rea and he burst out laughing as she began to struggle in his arms, her small face glowing with embarrassment—temper—

confusion. Burke was doing this deliberately to impress Iris, and it hurt Rea when she remembered how he had rejected her from his arms, only the night before, having no audience to impress.

"Put me down, Burke! Oh, put me down!" She pummelled his shoulders. "I'm not Peter—and I'm not a pink elephant! Put me down!"

"I don't want to." He blew at her fringe. "You're mine to do exactly what I like with."

"Heavens, Tab, doesn't he sound a regular caveman?" Iris remarked, her laughter now a trifle off-key, the fingernails of her right hand digging into the back of the couch. Tab watched her hand, the claw-like tension of it, and he fought a sudden compassionate urge to take hold of that hand, to ease open the clenched fingers and soothe it back to calmness in his own warm hand. He knew that jealousy was storming in her, wrenching her nerves to pieces, and with a muffled sigh he rose to his feet and said to her: "It's pretty late, Iris. It might be a good idea if we made a move. I've got my car, I'll drive you home."

"Yes, all right." She pulled her hand away from the couch and looked at it as though it hurt her.

"We'll be dashing, then, Burke," Tab said.

"Right!" With a laugh Burke swung Rea to her feet. "There you are, my love, now you can do your duties as a hostess."

With flushed cheeks and disarranged hair, Rea walked to the door, followed by Iris. As they went up the stairs, Iris glanced sideways at Rea's dress. "So Burke took you shopping while you were in London, my dear?" she remarked. "What did you think of Madame Baum? I know that little number you've got on is one of hers."

"I liked her," Rea said. "She was awfully kind."

"Oh, she would be!" Iris laughed her silken and slightly malicious laughter. "Madame likes rich customers. I guessed, of course, that Burke wouldn't let you run round like a schoolgirl indefinitely. He likes smart clothes." Her eyes slipped assessingly over Rea. Then she said, one hand attractively pressed against the swell of her right breast: "What a pity you're so slight, Rea. You've hardly any bosom, though I must admit you don't look bad in that little dress. Of course, it's beautifully cut; that makes a difference." Her glance rested on Rea's wrist. "Jewellery, too, I see! Burke is a generous husband!"

"Y-yes." Rea flushed slightly, pressing her wrist against her side, as though she would hide the little watch from Iris's curiosity. There was a hard glitter in the jade eyes now, an open revealing of the antagonism and dislike which Iris hid in front of other people. They entered Rea's bedroom and Iris swung gracefully into her fur coat and wound a shining scarf about her hair. Then she turned from the dressing-table, her eyes roving round the big, dark, but beautiful room, in which Rea, standing rather tense against one of the carved posts of the bed, looked indisputably lost—a willow-slim figure in amber, her short fair hair still dishevelled from her tussle with Burke.

"For someone who says she can't play cards, you've played yours remarkably well haven't you, my dear?" Iris drawled. Her glance shifted to the big bed, moved over it, deliberately. "You little shopgirls and typists must know a thing or two—though, of course, Burke was always inclined to seek amorous occupation outside his own social circle. It was little farm-girls at one time, you know."

"That's a horrible thing to say!" Rea gasped.

"Nevertheless true, dear." Irish brushed nonchalantly at one of the gleaming sleeves of her mink. "Nevertheless true."

"Dani Larchmont wasn't just a little farm-girl," Rea said fiercely, remembering the wonderful face of the girl, the daring laughter in the lovely, slanting eyes. "She was perfectly beautiful! If Burke l-liked her, who could blame him?"

"Not you, evidently." Iris's eyes went narrow as they travelled Rea's suddenly passionate face. She looked, Iris thought, with scornful amusement, like some small tigress roused to swift protection of its young. "So Burke can do no wrong in your eyes, Rea? No wonder this marriage appeals to him! Not only a wife who's accommodating, but one who throws in adoration as well! Well, make the most of him while you have him; with his restless temperament there's no knowing how long he'll be satisfied with this little trip of his into the land of nymphs and gnomes." Iris's smile was vividly spiteful in that moment. "You have that kind of face, dear; did you know? It puts one immediately in mind of funny little people sitting on the tops of toadstools."

And yours, Rea thought, with a sudden rush of deep resentment as she followed Iris from the room, puts me in mind of a jealous cat's!

Tab and Burke had left the library and were waiting for Iris out on the front step. "Mr. Ryeland has gone up to bed," Tab said. "I bade him goodnight for you, Iris."

"Then let us be off." She shared a dazzling smile between Rea and Burke. "Goodnight, my children, we'll leave you to your play." She ran down the steps, holding out her hand to Tab, and her face in the streaming light from the hall was the vividly animated face of an actress taking a final curtain call. "Come along, my dear doctor, let us share the stars and the silent night."

"Now there's an invitation, old man," Burke laughed.

"It has a sting," Tab retorted. "Iris knows that my car is so ancient I need both hands to drive with." He joined Iris at the bottom of the steps, turning to lazily wave good night. Then he assisted Iris into his rather dilapidated coupé and they drove off, leaving behind them a small cloud of blue fumes.

It was a soft, bright night for so late in the year, and Tab remarked on the fact. Iris made no reply to his remark and he shot a quick glance at her profile, clear and rather white in the light of the dashboard. "Stop it, Iris!" The words crisped out of his mouth, sudden anger at the back of them. "Burke doesn't want you, Iris. He never has wanted you. Learn to accept and to live with that and you'll outgrow this terrible and exhausting passion of yours. Perhaps you'll even come to accept the fact that there are other men in the world, ready, willing and able to give you the worship you'll never get from Burke Ryeland. He belongs to Rea—to Rea, do you hear?"

"Don't—don't keep saying it!" She shivered, violently, and a convulsive expression of sheer pain turned ugly for a fleeting moment the chiselled vividness of her face. "You're cruel, Tab! Cruel!"

"I'd like to be kind!" Suddenly his voice was husky with feeling. "My God, how I'd like to be kind to you, Iris—if you would only let me!"

There was a moment of silence, which Iris finally broke with laughter. "You're Tab Gresham, therefore you might as well be at the North Pole for all I care," she said carelessly. She reached to him and mockingly patted his arm. "I shall have to look around and find you a nice pussycat." One of her slender chestnut eyebrows rose in a playful peak. "There's little Rea Ryeland—would you like her? She's nicely housebroken, and she purrs when you smile at her and give her a pat on the head."

"Rea Ryeland," Tab returned deliberately, "is the nicest girl I've ever met. She's very kind and absolutely genuine."

"Genuine?" The word slid slyly out of Iris's mouth. "Now I don't think so. I think there's something very, very funny about Burke's young bride."

"Funny?" Tab shot a suddenly uneasy glance at Iris's profile. "What makes you say that?"

"Several things." She examined the long fingernails of her left hand, pushing at the half-moon on her middle finger. "She's half Burke's age, plain as a plate, and she goes all colours of the rainbow when you happen to mention—Peru. Now why should she do that? Please tell me, Tab. I'm curious."

Tab's hands tightened on the wheel of the car. So Iris, too, was doubting that story of Burke's, that he and Rea had met while he had been in Peru? Lord, it wouldn't do for Iris to get too curious! She wanted Burke and she was unscrupulous, and though Tab loved her, he knew her capability for cruelty. Little Rea, caught in Iris's talons, would be rent to pieces! Tab winced at the thought.

"You're talking rot, you know," he said quietly, steering Iris into a channel that would take her questing mind off that Peru business. "Rea isn't as plain as a plate, unless you're talking about Chelsea porcelain."

"Chelsea porcelain! My dear Tab, I think you've blown your hooter!" Iris lay back against the worn beige leather of Tab's car and shook with laughter. Yet it was laughter, Tab noticed, with a definite edge of wildness to it. "The poor little ninny is as plain as a dinner-plate! It's perfectly obvious why Burke married her — he wanted someone who wouldn't intrude too often on his precious isolation!" Then Iris's laughter died on a sharp note; a note with tears and anger in it. "Damn him! Damn him for playing the fond fool with her—in front of me!"

"He's her husband," Tab remarked mildly.

"For now!" Iris sat up, pulling her fur coat about her body with a sudden seductive movement. "For now he's that!"

"Iris!" Tab spoke now with a tired exasperation. "Iris, you're a lovely girl; you've the world to choose from. Forget Burke—do yourself a favour."

"Tell me to forget that I live and breathe," Iris retorted.

CHAPTER TWELVE

THE branches of the great yew arched fantastically from the gnarled trunk and touched the ground, where, like snaking arms, they reached forward to the little lych gate across the path to the village church, the church built on Mendip rock, with a dazzling angel figure in its east window, where the Ryelands had their family pew and their stone memorials to their many ancestors.

This road to the village, almost a private one, for it led direct from King's Beeches, rarely brought Rea in contact with people. Occasionally a farm cart might trundle past and the weather-beaten driver call out a greeting to her, recognizing her as 'old maister's granddaughter-in-law.' Or a solitary cow might come ambling along, thrusting its nose in the hedges and rolling an inquisitive eye in Rea's direction. But today, as Rea stood before the old yew, her hands thrust into the pockets of her coat and her head a little to one side as she surveyed the tree, sauntering yet purposeful footsteps suddenly approached behind her, ringing loud in the quiet.

Rea swung round, her mouth making an O of startled surprise, even perhaps of slight nervousness, as her eyes discovered Jack Larchmont.

He stood before her, handsome and slender and disreputable-looking, his taunting grin lifting one corner of his mouth. He gestured at the tree. "In ancient days a wizard, wouldn't you say?" he drawled. Then he stepped to the lych gate and rested one booted leg upon it, his hands in the pockets of his ancient breeches. "Say hullo to me," he coaxed, deliberately moving his slanting eyes over her face.

"H-hullo." Rea's own hands were suddenly clenched in her pockets and she could feel her cheeks growing warm. She pulled her glance away from the taunting mesmerism of Jack's. "This is a fantastic tree, isn't it?" She tried to speak lightly. "I—I suppose I'm bound to be impressed by such things, being a Londoner."

"Little London sparrow." The words came softly, and Rea drew back a little, definitely uneasy now. "I'm fond of London," Jack drawled, "but I don't get much chance to see it. A busy, busy farm boy, that's me."

Rea smiled slightly. "You don't appear to be very busy at the moment," she said.

"True. Very true." His grin deepened. "Would it interest you to know that I was up all last night, playing midwife to a cow?" Then he burst out laughing at the expression of open scepticism on her face. "You haven't a very flattering opinion of me, have you, little girl?"

"Well, you said yourself that your proper guise was horns and hoofs," she retorted.

"Ah, so I did, so I did. All the same, little girl, it's true about the cow. Her name is Julie and she's sweet and gentle as a May morning. I like sweet, gentle things, surprisingly enough, but they're so hard to find. When one does find them, they always seem to belong to other people. Sad, isn't it?"

"Is it?" Rea scuffed the ground with the toe of her shoe, not fully understanding him.

"It's terrible. Of course, one could always reach out and grab what one wants, regardless of the owner. Shall I do that, Rea?"

She was so startled that he knew her name that the full implication of his question passed her by. "How do you know my name?" she demanded.

"Why, I know your maid," he drawled. "Little Betty. Hasn't she ever mentioned me? She often mentions you. She tells me the most interesting things about you."

"Betty?" Rea gazed up at him with big, startled eyes. "W-what does she tell you?"

"Oh," he considered, chipping at the lichen on the yew with the nail of his right forefinger, "various amazing things. Servants are inquisitive creatures, Rea; their sharp eyes don't miss a thing."

"What should Betty miss?" Rea faced him in a sudden flash of anger. "You've no right to question her about me! What has she been saying to you?"

"She's been saying that your husband is a most unusual man."

"Unusual—Burke?" Rea was watching Jack Larchmont in a rather frightened fashion now. Servants, as he said, were inquisitive creatures, and Betty, with her cowlike eyes under her low-worn cap, was inclined to snoop. Until the advent of Rea's new clothes from London, Rea had often caught her examining the meagre contents of her wardrobe and her chest-of-drawers, as though it puzzled her that the wife of a rich man like Burke Ryeland should be so lacking in fine dresses and expensive underwear.

"Yes, unusual," Jack Larchmont reiterated. "I call it unusual for a man not to share his wife's bed."

The words hung between them in the ensuing silence, blatant and unlovely. Rea blushed hotly, and then went very white. "How dare you say that!" she gasped. "How dare you discuss my husband with a—a servant!"

Jack Larchmont greeted this with a mocking smile. "Why? Is he some sort of a divinity? Mustn't his name be used on the coarse lips of the hoi-polloi?"

"You're horrible!" Rea gasped. "Listening to Betty's low gossip—encouraging it! Putting your own vile interpretation upon things she's told you—things she can't possibly know anything about!" Rea's hazel eyes flashed as they met the dark mockery of his eyes. "I have a son, remember? Does the inquisitive Betty suggest that I found my Peter under a—a gooseberry bush?"

"He's neither your Peter—nor the gallant Burke's!" Jack drawled. Then, like the tongue of a snake striking, his hand swooped upon Rea's wrist. He held her a prisoner as he stepped close to her. "I heard what my father said to you that day you came to our farmhouse, but I knew long before that that Philip Ryeland wasn't the little white god everyone thought him—a case of raven recognizing raven, I guess." The slanting eyes glittered as they held Rea's, mesmerizing her, filling her with revolt and fear. That he should know! That he should know—this wild, unscrupulous gipsy creature, so soured by the unhappiness that lay over his house! "We've not met by moonlight," he said, very softly, "but the horns and hoofs are out, Rea. I said you should see them, didn't I?"

"I'm seeing them," she returned, the skin of her face so taut and cold that she knew she had gone white. "I was foolish enough to feel sorry for you the other day, but now I only dislike you. I think you're out to make mischief."

"Oh, but that depends on you," he laughed. His fingers tightened on her wrist, pulling her hand up his jersey-clad breast. "I don't intend that you should dislike me, Rea. I might promise to keep several Ryeland secrets, if you promise to be my—friend."

"W-what does that mean?" Rea searched his eyes uneasily. "Don't talk in riddles, tell me outright what you mean!"

"And offend your very patent modesty, little girl?" His grin was slow, full of devilry, while his eyes roved her face. "You haven't the know-all of a week-old kitten, have you? Wife and mother! It's laughable!" Then his eyes grew suddenly narrow with curiosity. "Did the gallant Burke actually marry you?"

Rea flushed hotly. "Of course he married me!"

"Of course he married you!" Jack mimicked. "Lend a little truth to the great lie, eh? Wow, there'd be hell to pay if the real truth came out, wouldn't there? The old man would sling all three of you out of the old ancestral home. What's Burke doing it for, the house and the money?"

"Burke—do that?" Rea was icy with contempt. "Do you think every man thinks with your kind of mind? Burke loves Peter, and his grandfather; he's doing it for them."

"How noble!" Jack sneered. "It wouldn't be because he played my sister a damn dirty trick once and thought this a good way to ease his conscience, bringing her kid here and calling it his?"

This came so dangerously close to the truth that Rea felt her heart turn over. "You mustn't say anything! You won't say anything, will you?" Her eyes were large with fear as they pleaded with him. "Burke means well, he really does. He loves Peter—and so does Mr. Ryeland. It would break Mr. Ryeland's heart if he found out the real truth. And nothing you can say can bring your sister back again—why, it can only dirty her name and—and probably kill your mother. Think of her, if you don't want to think of anyone else. You love her; I know you love her."

"But love is an empty emotion when it's one-sided, Rea. It embitters, empties the heart of the desire to do right, only fills it with a devilish urge to do wrong." His warm, hard fingers pressed Rea's small hand over his heart. "It beats, Rea, my heart , and it feels—but it feels things it shouldn't. It feels that it wants another man's wife—and it knows that it's going to have her. Now look shocked, feel shocked, and act shocked. Display all the conventional reactions, but don't forget that I hold the reputations of the Ryeland clan in the palm of my hand. It rests with you whether or not I disclose what I know. I care not about breaking my own mother's heart, for you can't break that which is already broken."

Abruptly he released Rea's hand and put her from him. "Think over what I've said, little girl. We'll meet again." Then he swung on his heel, his sauntering footsteps slowly dying away—dying away, the rural stillness closing down about Rea.

She shivered violently, like a sleeper waking from a bad dream, and slowly turned her footsteps back towards King's Beeches. That Jack Larchmont should know—that he should know! Wild as a gipsy, dark as a devil, tormented and tormenting! What was she to do? What was she to do?

A leaf fell from a tree behind her, ran with a soft patter at her heels, and suddenly she was running—running from her frightened thoughts and the drawling menace of Jack's voice.

She had tea in the nursery, with Moira and Peter, and their company successfully obliterated Jack Larchmont from her mind for a while. But at dinner that evening, sitting across the table from Burke and listening in a desultory fashion to the rather technical conversation he was holding with his grandfather on the merits and demerits of mechanical ploughing and sowing, it all came rushing back. And foremost upon the tide came that unlovely remark of Jack's: "I call it unusual for a man not to share his wife's bed."

Rea quickly lowered her eyes to her plate, cutting at her gooseberry tart almost desperately. How dared he say such a thing! How dared Betty gossip and give him room to say it! She lifted a small piece of tart to her mouth and chewed it without tasting it. Whatever would Burke's grandfather think if this piece of kitchen gossip reached his ears . . . ?

Then she jumped, realizing that Burke had addressed a remark to her. "I—I beg your pardon?" She gazed across the table at him, completely unaware that her eyes still held a frightened reflectiveness.

"What's the matter, Rea? Why are you looking like that?" Burke slowly lowered his wine-glass from his lips, his eyes moving questioningly over her face.

"L-like what?" Her fork clattered nervously against her plate and she was uncomfortably aware of the irritated little tut-tut Mr. Ryeland made.

"Well, sweetie," one of Burke's black eyebrows drew down and a slightly sardonic smile went across his face, "you looked just as though I'd just caught you rifling the family silver—or planning to. Now drink up your wine, we don't want to be at the table all night."

She reached for her wine-glass, and then gave a sharp little cry of dismay. The stem, thin and delicate as gossamer, had slipped out of her hand and now the wine-glass lay in pieces on the floor—the priceless Venetian glass, shredded with faint lines of gold, was gone to nothing in a pool of golden, spreading wine.

Rea scrambled from her chair, her great frightened eyes fixed upon the taut anger of old Mr. Ryeland's face. "I'm sorry—I'm sorry!" she gasped. Then childishly, quick tears of both fright and embarrassment trembling on her lashes, she crouched down by the breakage and began to pick the shards of glass out of the wine.

"Pack that up, Rea!" Burke was round the table in a couple of strides, brusquely lifting her to her feet. He saw blood running down one of her fingers and gave a curt exclamation. "You little fool, what did you want to go messing about with the glass for?" He dragged a handkerchief from his pocket and began to mop at the finger, while his grandfather said cuttingly: "Do you realize, miss, that you've just smashed an irreplaceable piece of family glass?"

Rea gulped, two great tears slowly rolling down her cheeks. "I'm sorry—I'm sorry!" she said again.

"Dash it all, miss, being sorry won't replace that wine-glass," Mr. Ryeland snapped.

"We're fully aware of that, sir," Burke broke in, winding his handkerchief about Rea's finger. "Rea didn't break the darn thing on purpose."

"She should learn to be more careful," his grandfather retorted. "She isn't living in some twopenny-halfpenny suburb now, drinking out of shilling tumblers from Woolworth's."

Burke glanced up sharply. "That was a damned unnecessary remark," he said.

"But none the less an accurate one, I take it?" A sneer crossed the elderly, autocratic face. "I fear it's that French blood in you gives you your somewhat plebeian tastes, my boy."

"Then thank God I have it, otherwise I might be like you!" Burke retorted crisply. Then he passed his arm about Rea's waist and marched her from the dining-room.

Burke snapped on the lights of his study and with a little sigh Rea went over to the fireplace and knelt on the Bokhara rug.

"Such a beautiful wine-glass," she murmured. "I should have been more careful—and he's right about shilling tumblers! Dad and I couldn't afford Venetian glass and specially imported wines." She turned her unhappy gaze away from the bright leap of the apple logs. Their piquant scent couldn't charm her tonight. "You shouldn't have brought me here, Burke," she said. "I'm all wrong—all wrong for this place! I knew I should be! I said so, didn't I?"

Burke watched her a moment, then abruptly he crossed the room to her, lifted her from the rug and sat down in an armchair with her. She was very slight in his arms, her arms suddenly locked about his neck in the shaken need of a hurt child to be comforted. This was not Burke, this comforting figure. This was her father, holding her when she fell and scraped her knees; holding her when he had to tell her that he was ill and not going to get well. She clung closely, absorbing the comfort that flowed out from the masculine shoulders, the strong arms, the mingled scents of cigarettes and after-shave lotion. After a while she whispered shakily: "I'm an awful baby, aren't I? I'm worse than little Peter cutting his teeth."

"You're a sensitive little cuss, that's all." Burke took her chin in his hand and tilted her face up to him. "Perhaps I shouldn't have brought you here, Rea. Living a lie doesn't rest easy with you, does it?"

Her lashes quivered, dropped down over her eyes, shielding them from Burke's searching gaze. "What would happen—if your grandfather ever found out?" she whispered.

"The shock might very well kill him," Burke returned uncompromisingly. "That's a chance I've had to take, all along. The happiness of a little boy on the one hand, the possibility of Grandfather discovering my duplicity on the other. I weighed the two, very carefully, right from the beginning, and I decided to put Peter's happiness first. The autocratic pride of the Ryelands brought about his birth, so why shouldn't they be the ultimate sufferers?"

Rea flinched at the sudden hard edge to Burke's voice, her tired, perplexed head pressing into his shoulder. She had no autocratic pride, only a young and frightened heart, a body that shrank from inflicting pain. She couldn't face with Burke's equanimity the thought of his grandfather's shattered life, should he ever learn that his beloved Philip had not been worthy of his great pride in him; that Peter was the living proof that Philip could stoop to debase a name he was supposed to worship, the ancient name of Ryeland. Old Mr. Ryeland had not shown her a real moment's kindness since she had been in this house, he openly despised her, but neither his unkindness nor his hate could alter what she decided there against the hard warmth of Burke's shoulder. Jack Larchmont would not blast either of the lives he had threatened, not if it lay in her power to turn him from that embittered purpose. Then, remembering his gipsy face, his glittering eyes, his fingers like burning wires about her wrist, she shivered violently.

Burke felt her shiver and rather anxiously touched her forehead. It was hot under his hand, and little flushes lay over the delicate curving of her cheekbones. "I believe you're starting a cold," he murmured.

"I—I'm all right." A slight smile flitted across her face. "It's breaking that wine-glass. It's given me a headache."

"Poor baby!" He brushed at her fringe, his eyes on the drooping curves of her mouth. He drew her a little closer, watching the defenceless way her head lay back against his arm, the young throat very white, the dark lashes, just tipped with gold, trembling on her slightly flushed cheeks. "Rea," he spoke gently, "would you like to go away from King's Beeches?"

"Away?" Her eyes flew wide open, while her arms involuntarily tightened about his neck. "Away from you —and Peter? Oh, no!"

"Are you sure, Rea?" He touched her cheek, following the curve of her cheekbone with his finger. "You don't seem all that happy here, and I don't feel I have the right to keep you, if you're not happy."

"I—I'm happy enough," she stammered. "I love Peter. I couldn't bear to be parted from him." Her hands pressed against the warmth of Burke's neck, almost pleadingly. "You don't want me to go away, do you, Burke?" she asked.

"Of course not, baby!" He dropped a quick kiss on her forehead. "I'd miss you terribly if you went away."

"Would you?" Her hazel eyes roved his face, a rather startled pleasure in them. "I didn't think you noticed me all that much." Then she thought of certain assorted ivory and salmon boxes that had arrived from London just a few short days ago. Oblong boxes; round boxes; all very exciting. She sat up in Burke's arms. She gave an excited little laugh, her depression momentarily forgotten. "You'll notice me next Saturday, though, when we go to Iris's birthday dance."

"When you're all dolled up in your grand new dress,

eh?" He grinned at her. "I thought you didn't want to outshine Iris?"

"Oh, I don't expect to outshine Iris," she said at once. "But I think you'll like my dress. It rustles."

"Rustles, eh?" His blue eyes held a lazy amusement as they rested on her soft cap of fair hair. He touched it, brushing it back from her pixie ears. "You're a nice child, aren't you, Rea?" he murmured.

"I—I'm not a child." She sat primly in his lap, her hands folded, and it seemed to her she was always telling him she wasn't a child.

"Nor a pink elephant, eh, to be played with?" He laughed down into her eyes. "Sweetie, I'm so much older than you that I'm bound to treat you as a child."

"You're thirty-six," she said, "and that isn't old. I wish I was thirty-six."

"Why?"

"I—I'd have more dignity—m-more knowledge of the world." She lowered her eyes from his, thinking of Jack Larchmont—and the things he had said.

"Age doesn't always bring wisdom, my dear," Burke said. "Though it often brings the disheartening knowledge of how unwise one has been." Then he rose to his feet and released her from his arms. "Get your book and have a little read, there's a good girl. I've got some paper work to get through tonight."

"Yes, Burke." She found her book and curled herself into one of the big wing-chairs, but she wasn't really reading. More often than not she was watching Burke at his big desk, his dark head bent over a businesslike array of beige-coloured forms, his absorption complete as he rapidly moved his pen.

So kind always—but so distant! Petting her sometimes, in a fond, abstract way. Unaware that the unhappiness he had glimpsed in her eyes tonight had for its basis a frightened recoil from the passion of another man. Rea shrank closer into the soft, wine-coloured upholstery of her chair as she remembered Jack's eyes—Jack's bold, slanting, wanting eyes. Her own breath seemed to catch in her throat as she seemed to feel Jack's quick, warm breath fanning her face again. She wanted to cry out to Burke: "Help me—help me!" but she didn't dare—she didn't dare.

Jack wouldn't hesitate to divulge all he knew about Peter's birth, recklessly spreading the story, if she sought to protect herself and thereby left Burke wide open to attack. Not only Burke but his grandfather and Mrs. Larchmont and the dead and lonely Dani Larchmont.

All attacked by scorn . . . sneered at . . .

Rea shuddered.

CHAPTER THIRTEEN

GONE was the usual bovine watchfulness from Betty's eyes, now they gleamed with a startled admiration. " 'Tis a rare sight you look, ma'am," she murmured with awe, studying Rea with her head on one side. "Like a fairy you are, an' that's a fact."

Rea gave an excited little laugh, stroking the silk rustling of her crimson and gold dress.

She studied herself in the mirror with an innocent, excited pleasure. The bare skin of her shoulders and her arms seemed to shine luminous against the flickering flame of the dress, and her hair, which had been washed earlier in the day, shone like a cap of gold from the vigorous brushing Betty had given it. Her lips were just faintly touched with lipstick, and once again the dress was lending a mysterious depth and promise to her eyes.

"Get my cloak, Betty," she said, and for a moment put a rather shaky hand to her midriff, where a couple of dozen butterflies seemed to be darting in all directions. Betty brought a black velvet cloak to Rea and helped her to adjust and fasten it. "Aren't you wearin' any jewellery, ma'am?" she asked.

Rea shook her head, smiling slightly. "I've only my watch, Betty," she said, "and I can't wear that with this dress." She made for the door, delighting in the silken rustle of her skirts.

"Have you a good time, ma'am," the girl said, looking rather shy again.

"Why, thank you!" Rea turned to give her maid a quick smile and for a moment they gazed at one another —and suddenly Betty, with her funny low-worn cap and bovine eyes, brought another presence into that room. Suddenly Jack Larchmont was in that room, leering dark and frightening over Betty's shoulder. Rea's happy smile faltered and like a small creature darting from the sudden sight of a trap she sped in her lovely dress and her sleek cloak from the big bedroom.

She hurried along to the nursery, for she had promised to let Moira see her in her finery before she departed for the dance. Moira couldn't admire the dress enough, circling around Rea, exclaiming and throwing up her hands. " 'Tis the belle of the ball you'll be, ma'am! 'Tis indeed! My, but I've never seen a prettier dress, not even on Miss Mallory."

The remark made Rea's eyes dance as she bent over Peter's cot to give him a kiss and a cuddle before she went. "Night-night, Peter boy. Say night-night."

He burbled a lot of delightful nonsense in reply and thrust up a one-eyed monkey for her to kiss. She gave it a peck, to Peter's plump delight, gave him a final hug and turned to rustle her way from the nursery. " 'Tis mighty proud of you young master will be this night," Moira remarked.

"Fine feathers, Moira!" Rea scoffed, and before the maid could answer her, she was skimming along the landing. She was way down the stairs before she realized that someone was standing below, watching her descent.

She watched Burke under her lashes, very splendid in his black evening clothes, his blue eyes sparkling with amusement as he stood waiting for her, one foot upon the bottom stair.

Then she was close to him and he was reaching for her, swinging her down the remaining three or four stairs. With cool, deliberate hands he removed her cloak and threw it over the newel-post of the stairs, then he held her at arm's length and studied her. "D'you think that ravishing dress deserves a present?" he queried.

"Oh, no!" She shook a quick, confused head. "No, Burke!"

"Oh, yes!" He laughed and turned her about in his arms. "Yes, Rea!" Then she felt his cool hands at her throat and when she glanced down she saw that he had fastened a slender gold chain about her throat, to which was attached a dainty little cameo.

Her fingers caressed it as she eagerly turned to face him. "Oh, Burke, this is lovely! How kind you are! Where did you get it?"

"I saw it in an antique shop in Taunton one day last week. I couldn't resist it, it reminded me so much of you—delicate, innocent, sweet." Then he laughed and reached out a hand to touch the sudden bloom of deep pink upon her cheek. "Why are you blushing?" he asked. "Don't you like receiving compliments?"

Her lashes trembled, then defeated by confusion they swept down over her eyes. A tremulous little laugh broke from her. "They're nice, but confusing," she said.

"Most women take to them like sleek young cats to cream," he drawled. He reached for her cloak and carefully fastened it about her. "We're attending the soirée on our own, by the way," he said. "Grandfather has decided to stop at home. He has those rheumatic pains in his legs again."

"Oh, what a shame!" Rea's eyes widened in quick sympathy.

They went out to the car, Burke carrying his coat over his arm. The night was cold, with a sky so clear that the tiny stars sparkled sharply, like frost motes. Rea drew her cloak about her, casting a rather worried glance at Burke. "Aren't you going to put your coat on?" she asked.

He shook his head, tossing the coat into the back of the car. He grinned as he turned to her, taking hold of her hand. "I don't feel the cold all that much. In you get."

The bonfire was already lit when they arrived at the party, enormous and incandescent, throwing light for miles around, it seemed to Rea. Burke parked the car and escorted her through the throng of guests already in the forecourt of the house, calling greetings with careless good humour, his arm thrown about Rea's waist. Rea envied him his ease and his self-possession. She was taut with nerves, now that they had arrived, very conscious of the inquisitive glances that were following their progress across the forecourt to where Iris stood in the streaming light of the wide-thrown glass doors of the ballroom, receiving her guests. Her father stood beside her, moustached and jovial, an almost fulsome pride in the girl at his side written upon his red, rather horsey face.

Rea had never seen Iris looking lovelier — or more pagan. Her gown, of a deep and glistening sea-green silk, was almost medieval in its simplicity of line; a line so uncluttered that every line and curve of Iris's perfect body was unashamedly revealed. The only jewellery she wore was a long, barbaric necklace of square-cut pieces of jade, exactly the colour of her eyes. She looked, Rea thought, like a princess out of some ancient tale of jousting, turbulent knights, who rode hard and loved hard and died at the whim of the gorgeous and arrogant Iris.

"Go along into the house, dear," she drawled at Rea. "You'll be shown where to put your wrap. I'm going to hang on to this husband of yours, if you don't mind."

Rea's eyes flew open in quick alarm. The thought of being suddenly alone among all these people, so incredibly assured as they strolled about the forecourt, laughing and talking and throwing gay compliments to Iris, made her want to throw her arms childishly about Burke's neck and cling like a limpet, defying anybody to wrench her free. He saw her alarm and bent to her with a smile. "It's all right, Rea, go along in and comb your fringe. I'll be waiting for you."

Rea was in the midst of combing her wind-tossed hair when she became aware of someone watching her through the cloakroom mirror. The woman was large and grey-haired and tanned, and Rea gave an involuntary smile at the energetic and extremely unfeminine manner in which she was applying powder to her craggy face. It was flying about in all directions. "Must take off some of the shine," she grunted at Rea. "Feel a bit of a fool, to tell you the truth. I'm better in the saddle than getting ready to gallop round a ballroom. I'm Rita Coe, by the way. Tell me, why hasn't Burke brought you to see me yet? Is he afraid you'll think my nags better than his?"

Rita Coe? Of course, that harum-scarum woman who ran a riding-school! Burke had often mentioned her. Rea's answering smile was a rather touching compound (Rita, who was a good-hearted woman, saw it) of shy gratitude for a friendly overture when she was feeling painfully awkward among a lot of strangers, and genuine interest in a friend of Burke's.

"Burke says you have a roan who is almost as fleet as Rebel, Mrs. Coe," she said shyly.

"Almost!" Rita's handsome grey eyes, the only handsome thing about her, flashed with indignation. "My Talleyrand can outpace that brutal devil of Burke's any day of the week. Got style, has my Tally. All that swine Rebel has got is a king-size temper." Then she suddenly grinned, thrusting her powder-puff into an old-fashioned beaded purse. "I will say Burke manages him beautifully. Fine horseman! Do you ride, child?"

Rea shook her head.

Mrs. Coe looked dumbfounded. "But you must ride, my child. We all ride. I'll have to talk to Burke about you, get him to send you to me." She stood back to appraise Rea. "You're thin, not a lot of strength in you, but you'll look well on a nice little black mare. Um, you're a pretty child. Burke said you were."

"Burke did?" Rea looked like a little girl caught at a keyhole as she stared at Rita Coe.

Rita gave her a quizzical look. "Hasn't he told you he thinks so?" Then, taking pity on Rea's young confusion, she added: "Come along, let's go and join the fray."

They left the cloakroom and strolled along the corridor that led back to the ballroom. "What do you think of Iris?" Mrs. Coe asked. "Handsome little cat, isn't she? We've given her a length of real Irish tweed for her birthday, Bill and I—Bill's my husband, you'll have to meet him. It's a splendid piece of stuff—God knows what she'll do with it! What did you give her?"

"A saddle. Burke brought it over yesterday."

Rita Coe frowned slightly as she glanced sideways at Rea. "You don't let him come over here too often on his own, do you? Don't do it, child! Don't do it! Iris likes Burke; perhaps you've heard?"

"I've seen." Rea's smile was impish.

Rita Coe gave a gruff laugh. "You're cool about Iris, I must say. Got that big boy under your thumb, have you?"

Rea laughed. "Hardly! But he's very attached to our —our baby. I'm not afraid."

"Good girl!" Rita's eyes gleamed appreciatively. "You've got gumption. You'll make a nice little horsewoman."

They reached the ballroom and crossed to the glass doors that led to the forecourt. The huge bonfire was throwing showers of red sparks into the sky, its dancing light softening and warming the severe grey frontage of Mallory Court, a myriad tiny bonfires reflecting in the many oblong windows of the house. People were everywhere, laughing, talking, impatiently awaiting the first sounds of music from the ballroom. Footmen were moving among the laughing groups with loaded trays of sandwiches and drinks, for supper wouldn't be eaten until after the firework display.

"Now I wonder where the devil Bill is?" Rita Coe said, moving into the throng and casting impatient glances left and right. "I bet he's off in some corner with some of the boys, playing cards or sampling a gin concoction of the Colonel's." She shot an enquiring glance at Rea over the rather manly proportions of her shoulder, swathed in wine-red velvet. "Can you see Burke?"

Rea shook her head, peering anxiously about.

"Well, you stay here," Rita said. "I'm going to find that husband of mine. I'm not having him galloping round that ballroom full of the Colonel's gin. You stay right here, I'll be back—with Bill in tow." She marched off, carrying the train of her velvet dress over her arm and showing such an inelegant amount of well-muscled calf that Rea burst out laughing.

"I quite agree," someone drawled behind her, "furiously funny, isn't she?"

Rea spun round and found herself gazing straight into the dark, taunting eyes of Jack Larchmont. He was lighting a cigarette and the flame of the lighter cast weird shadows over his face, turning it into a devil mask for Rea. Then he snapped the lighter shut and dropped it into his pocket. He was wearing dark evening dress and his blue-black hair was no longer unruly, it lay flat and neat, gleaming in the dancing light of the bonfire. He took a couple of puffs at the cigarette, his eyes wandering with slow, insolent pleasure over Rea's small face, now wiped utterly free of laughter. Now there was sharp fear in it, and open surprise that he should be here. He laughed softly. "Why, yes," he drawled, "I mix with the élite, just as I mix with their maids. That's the prerogative of a scapegrace."

Then, with great deliberation, he reached out and took hold of her right hand, pulling her towards him. "Let's get away from the crowd," he said, and his arm slid round her waist as he led her through the gay throng, uncaring of who might see, making for the shadow of tall cedars at the side of the house. Rea moved with him like an automaton, sick and cold with apprehension, knowing his intention and shrinking from it with every fibre of her young body. She wanted to scream out to him not to touch her — but she didn't dare— she didn't dare!

And there, in the deep shadow of the tall cedars, he tossed his half-smoked cigarette from him and swept her young, shaking body into his arms. He laid his face against her throat and whispered: "I adore you! I never stop thinking about you! Don't you care? Don't you care, little Rea? I lie awake at night, torn with wanting you. That's never happened to me before. I've never loved like this before. Oh, Rea, Rea, you drive me mad. I've got to have you—I'm going to have you!" His lips travelled her face, hot and wild, forcing a broken little sob from her as they closed upon her lips.

For wild seconds she drowned in the slaking demand of his kiss, shot through with an hysterical fear at the bruising closeness of his body—and then fear flowered into panic and she began to fight him, pushing her hands against his face, feeling that she would die or go mad if he didn't release her.

And then, shattering the moment—one of deep exultation for Jack Larchmont, one of deep horror for Rea—came footsteps on the fallen leaves of the cedars, a crisp voice, lashing Rea's heart. "You can let go of my wife, Larchmont," it said, "unless you want a broken neck."

Rea felt Jack go tense, then slowly he dropped his arms away from her trembling body. He turned to Burke, stood slender and poised before him, running a hand over his black hair. Rea saw his white teeth flash in an insolent smile. "Don't break my neck, Ryeland," he drawled. "Your wife wouldn't like it. My neck is very precious to her."

"You insolent swine!" Burke took a sudden quick step towards Jack, but he didn't retreat. He thrust his hands into the pockets of his dinner jacket and stood offering himself, with laughter, to a strength that was capable of breaking him in two if it wished. Rea, seeing this and full of fear that Burke might use his great strength, went running between the two men. She thrust restraining hands against Burke's chest. "No, don't!" she cried. "Don't do it, Burke!"

He stared down at her for a long moment, then he said, a scornful, cutting edge to his voice: "Put away your tears and relax, my dear. I'll not rob you of his precious neck." Then he swung on his heel and strode away, leaving Rea with a face that had gone waxen white. When Jack Larchmont would have put a hand upon her arm, she shrank from him in disgust and loathing. "I should have let him kill you!" she gasped. "That would have settled everything, stilled your tongue for ever!"

"Why didn't you, then, honey?" The slanting eyes mocked her. "Afraid for his neck?" He put back his gleaming black head and laughed loudly. "Well, your goose is cooked, well and truly cooked, in that direction, so I'd advise you to lose any affection you might have for his neck. You're going to give all your affection to me—I insist on it."

"I've only hate to give you!" she cried, and then she was running from him, running from the shadow of the cedars, back towards the fiery glow of the big bonfire.

Rea stood by the wide-thrown glass doors of the ballroom, her tormented eyes searching the dancers for Burke. She saw him—and caught her breath. He held Iris in his arms and he was laughing down into her vivid face, all sign of the anger and scorn that had blazed upon his face, under the grim cedars, quite gone, wiped away as though it had never been. Now his face wore only enjoyment, a frank admiration of the girl in his arms.

Rea drew a quick little sigh and turned away—bumping straight into Tab Gresham. He laughed and caught hold of her. "Whoa there! Where are you going in such a hurry? I want to dance, lady. Aren't you going to oblige?"

She raised her white face to him, her soft mouth working, trying to frame a coherent reply. She didn't want him to know there was anything wrong. If he asked questions, showed sympathy, she would burst into tears—and tears were perilous things, they loosened the tongue. She might, with tears pouring from her aching heart, tell this man things that mustn't be told.

"I—I was going to the bonfire," she lied wildly.

"To throw yourself on it?" He was still laughing, though he had now noticed her distress and was puzzled by it. His glance went past her shoulder and rapidly scanned the ballroom. He saw Burke, with Iris in his arms, and his eyes narrowed. So that was the trouble! The poor kid was hurt because Burke was dancing with Iris! Tab's warm heart responded to the hurt in Rea, for a similar hurt was in himself.

Iris was looking very lovely tonight, a medieval princess, caring only for the admiration of one man—the man who danced with her, laughed with her. His own admiration she scorned, just as she had seemed to scorn his birthday present. Yet now she was wearing his present, he saw. Wearing it because the jade pieces exactly reflected the colour of her eyes!

He took hold of Rea's hand. "I'm claiming my waltz, Rea. Come along," he said.

CHAPTER FOURTEEN

WHEE! The first big rocket shot high into the air and exploded loudly in a shower of multi-coloured stars. And as though this were the signal for a general chaos to begin, Colonel Mallory and half a dozen riotous friends came running from around the side of the house, dragging a barrow on which sat a great straw-stuffed Guy Fawkes, its mangel-wurzel head leering from under a big bowler hat and its straw body clothed in an old hunting outfit of the Colonel's.

"Where's Iris?" one of the men called out. "She's got to see old man Fawkes launched on the bonfire."

"Yes, where's Iris?" another voice chimed in.

"We want Iris! We want Iris!" chanted the group as they drew the barrow to the blazing edge of the bonfire.

Tab Gresham, watching the scene with Rea and the Coes, frowned heavily as the boisterous cry for Iris grew louder and louder. He hadn't seen anything of Iris for at least half an hour—nor had he seen anything of Burke. The thought of them together, perhaps somewhere in the garden, perhaps somewhere in the great barrack of a house, deliberately seeking seclusion from everybody, sent the blood in a hot, angry wave to Tab's head. How dared she do it—how dared he do it! What of Rea? Standing like a little white statue in her pretty dress, knowing, just as he knew, that the loud chant for Iris wouldn't be answered in any great hurry—if she were with Burke.

Tab bit at his lip, aware of a clammy forehead, an irritating trickle of moisture against his right temple. He took out his handkerchief and wiped his forehead, and Rita Coe laughed as she glanced at him, the fierce light of the bonfire dancing red on her rugged features. "What's the matter, Doc, feeling the heat?" she asked. Then her grey eyes switched from his face and enthusiastically followed the green and purple progress of a stream of comet-like fireworks, cutting a gay arc through the sky. "Oh, that was a nice sight! Did you see them, Rea?"

"W-what?" Rea glanced hurriedly at Rita, pulling her wandering thoughts back to the party.

"Here's Iris!" Bill Coe suddenly exclaimed. "Look, they're going to burn the guy! They're lifting him off the barrow! Whoops, the Colonel nearly went in the fire himself! I say, I believe the old boy's tipsy, his nose is as red as a beet!"

Came high-spirited yells from across the forecourt, a loud cry of: "The Queen is here, boys, forward with the execution. Up with him, ready, steady,—and on he goes!" The straw arms and legs of the guy flailed wildly as the boisterous group of "executioners" tossed him into the flames, raising a loud cheer as he sank and immediately took fire.

Rea stood tense at Tab Gresham's side, her eyes fixed upon Iris, her shaking fingers locked upon the cameo at her throat. Where had Iris been—and what made her eyes shine so jewel-bright, catching and holding the soaring pyramid of the bonfire as she watched, surrounded by laughing men, the quick and crackling demise of Guy Fawkes?

And—and where was Burke?

Rea pressed her throat, as though to stifle the frightened little sobs that were clamouring there, struggling to escape. He hadn't come anywhere near her, hadn't even looked at her since that scene under the cedars, but he had danced several times with Iris—and during the course of those dances Rea had been constantly, painfully aware of Iris's triumphant glance upon her, the way she clung close to Burke, brilliant with her knowledge that he was deliberately devoting the evening to her. A situation which could have aroused comment among Iris's other guests, had Rea been left to play the wallflower while Burke danced. But she wasn't. Her waltz with Tab exhibited her in her slim flame of a dress and directly the waltz ended, several young men, like dark moths in their dark evening wear, clustered to Rea's flame silk and demandingly took her dance programme into their hands. "I—I'd rather not—I'm not much of a dancer!" she gasped, trying to escape them, but finding herself, in her shyness, inevitably captured by each young man in turn and whirled on to the long, crowded dance floor.

Now she stood in the forecourt, unwarmed by the dancing closeness of the big bonfire, alone as she had never felt alone in all her life before—though she stood with Tab, and her two new friends, Rita and Bill Coe. Her fingers found the chain of Burke's cameo and sudden tears swam thick into her eyes, blurring the image of Iris, so tall and queenly in her glistening green gown and plainly strung to a pitch of intense excitement. Rea shivered, for it seemed to her that Iris's eyes had caught fire from a heart fired with triumph.

She was unaware that Iris Mallory had begun to cross the forecourt towards her.

And as Iris came, her silk gown whispered about her legs and her jade necklace flashed like so many angry eyes—and words pounded in her mind. Words—spoken to Burke. Words that lashed her pride as she recalled them.

She and Burke had been dancing, and all at once, needing to speak, wanting to speak, triumphantly certain she ought to speak, now that he showed Rea this new, significant coldness, she had drawn him out to the terrace and there in the shifting gold and blue and emerald glow of softly swaying lanterns, she had bared her heart to him.

"Oh, Burke, do you really think I'm fooled?" she had said, laughing to think anyone could have been fooled. "I know you don't love that funny little Rea—how could you? I've seen how you've looked at her tonight, you despise her, you don't love her!" Her warm, bronzed hands had crept to his shoulders, the tips of her oval fingernails just touching the sides of his neck "Get rid of her, Burke! We can be together then. We were born to be together, you and I. We're part of the same soil, the same air, the same wind and rain. I want you, my dear, and we can be together for always, if you'll only throw that stupid little schoolgirl out of your life." With abrupt abandon her arms had closed about his neck. "I'm real—real, my dear! I'm not a puling miss!" And knowing her own vital and unashamed beauty in that moment, she had been certain of his answer, his response to all that she offered . . .

She had been stunned, horrified, when he had pushed her from him. She could hardly credit his crisp, contemptuous refusal of all she offered. "We've always been friends, Iris, and that needn't alter," he had said. "But I don't want your body. I never have."

"I'm giving you my heart—my heart!" she had cried.

"The two are surely one, to a woman!" he had retorted, and then he had swung on his heel and left her alone. Left her alone, love sinking down, down, joining the hate she knew for Rea . . .

She watched Rea, her cat-green glance of hate stealing over the slight figure, small, tense profile framed against the dancing red light of the bonfire. Then Iris's wary glance shifted to Tab Gresham, standing quiet beside Rea, bending his head to say something to her, presumably about the noisy, galloping Rita Coe, for he pointed to her. Iris was so close now that she heard Rea give a little chuckle in answer to what Tab said to her, but neither were aware of Iris behind them. Neither knew that with a sphinx-like inscrutability she bent to the bonfire, igniting the fuse of a small firework. Neither knew that as she straightened it flashed from her hand.

Perhaps she meant merely to frighten Rea—perhaps not, but one thing was certain—as the noise of the exploding firework crashed out behind Rea and she swung round in startled alarm, the dancing skirts of her dress were suddenly snatched into the hungry maw of the bonfire.

The first wild screams came from Rita Coe. She saw the real flame licking up the silken flame and in the nightmare moment her mouth tore open to release its horrified screams, a slender, black-clad figure leapt past her, grabbed hold of Rea and began to beat and tear at the flaming silk of her dress. His bare hands wrung out flame as though it were water, and just before a flooding darkness took hold of Rea and bore her away from nightmare, she looked into the night-black eyes of Jack Larchmont—night-black and agonized, filling Rea with a great wonderment as she fell into the darkness that swamped fear and horror and the tongues of flickering heat that this wild-eyed man took into his hands and snatched, from her arms, her face . . .

A man raced into the card-room, his rough handling of the door and his hasty footsteps breaking into the calm silence of the four men playing poker. "Ryeland! I say, Ryeland, you'd better come!" The man hurried to the table. "There's been an accident, old chap. It's your wife—her frock caught alight!"

Burke turned in his chair to stare up at the man. "What?"

"Your wife—her frock caught alight . . ."

"Her—frock—Dear God!" Burke's chair, a heavy oaken thing, spun from his hand like matchwood as he leapt to his feet. His poker hand sprayed the table and his card companions had one flashing, cinematic glimpse of his horrified face before he turned and went from the room at a run.

The corridor leading out to the forecourt seemed endless, and as he came out upon the stone flags, his face, in the flaring, writhing, red and gold light of the giant bonfire, showed naked and dark and full of perhaps the first real fear he had ever known in his life. He crossed the forecourt in long strides, and the silent crowd opened to let him through to where Tab Gresham and Rita Coe knelt on the ground beside Rea.

She lay as crumpled and crushed as a misused flower, a man's jacket covering the scorched remnants of her dress, her head pillowed upon Rita Coe's arm.

Tab glanced up at Burke. "Thanks to Larchmont here," he gestured at Jack, who stood to one side, his burned hands thrust out of sight behind his back, "she isn't badly hurt or marked. He beat out the flames."

"How did it happen?" Burke knelt beside Rea, staring down at her lax, crumpled little body, a nerve pulsing hard in his jaw as he reached out an unsteady hand and gently stroked the tumbled hair back from her forehead. She didn't stir, her lashes lying very still on her cheeks, and an impotent wildness lit Burke's eyes as he raised them to Tab. "My God, how did it happen? Doesn't anyone know?" He turned his head, gazing round at the silent crowd.

Tab did the same, and for a long instant his eyes dwelt on Iris, standing in the circle of her father's arm. His nerves, his instinct, told him something that his heart and his reason shrank from. But he couldn't forget the look her face had worn in that horrifying instant when Rita Coe's screams had turned his attention to Rea, a band of flame encircling the skirt of her dress. Iris's face had flashed out at him from the crowd—and it had worn a dark mask of overriding hate, the green eyes completely empty of the horror and distress so suddenly in the eyes of everyone else.

Hate, intense and passionate, for little Rea—Burke's wife—who had probably never hurt a soul in all her young life.

"I imagine," he said quietly, bending again over Rea's slight figure, "that she moved a little too close to the fire. Ah, she's coming round—see her lashes move, Burke?" He took Rea's hands into his own and gently rubbed them. He spoke carefully, softly to her, as to a frightened child: "It's all right now, Rea. All right now. There's no need to be afraid any more. Burke's here. He's going to take you home."

Colonel Mallory heard what he said and leant forward, touching his shoulder. "My house is at Mrs. Ryeland's disposal, Tab. Let her stay here."

But Tab shook a quick head, not looking up in case his eyes met the green eyes of Iris. "No. Rea will be better in her own home," he said. "I'll borrow some blankets if I may, though. And if you've any brandy . . ."

"Naturally! Naturally!" The Colonel went at a half-run across the forecourt, only too anxious to relieve some of the distress of this unfortunate occurrence. Poor child—she might have been killed—might have been killed! He mopped at his red face with a big handkerchief as he ran, calling out: "Benyon! Benyon, where the devil are you? Ah, good fellow, excellent! I'll take that brandy! Now run back to the house and fetch some blankets—hurry, man." The Colonel came hurrying back to Tab with the tray his butler had foresightedly brought out, a decanter of brandy and several glasses upon it.

Tab took one of the glasses and poured a generous finger of brandy into it, then he gently raised Rea's head and coaxed her to drink the brandy. She shuddered against his arm as the brandy moved down her throat, waking her back to reality, to remembrance of tall flames rising to embrace her. A sob broke from her, then another, and wearied and frightened, almost desperate for the shield and the solace of Burke's arms, she pulled away from Tab and reached blindly for Burke, tears breaking from her as he gathered her close to him. Then he lifted her and carried her through the watching crowd.

He made straight for his car, and impatient of Benyon and his blankets, carefully wrapped Rea in the heavy folds of the overcoat he had scorned to wear on the drive over. He pulled the big collar well up about her throat, feeling her tears rain warm upon his hands.

Overhead, clouds were marching across the face of the moon like an army on the move, portentously casting shadows as they went, darkening Burke's face and eyes to a remote hardness as he slid into the car beside Rea and carefully backed it out from among the other cars. He swung it to face the curve of the drive and they shot forward with a small roar into the night.

The wheels swished on the silent road and the headlights picked out the tall hedges and the darting rabbits below the hedges. Rea lay dazed and spent beside Burke, glad to the soul of her when the car at last drew in against the stone steps below the front door of King's Beeches.

Burke left her while he ran up the steps to pull the bell and summon Tolliver. Then he came back for her. He lifted her and carried her up the steps, and Rea, unable to bear his terrifying silence any longer, whispered brokenly: "Please, oh, please, don't be angry, Burke! Please! I can't bear it!"

"Angry?" His blue eyes came down to her, blazing out of the stone mask of his face. "I'm not angry, Rea."

"Then why—why do you look at me . . ."

"I'm not angry," he said again. The door opened and he brushed past Tolliver, carrying Rea into the hall. As Tolliver closed the door and then turned to stare at

Burke, with Rea so mute and white-faced in his arms, Burke said curtly: "There's been a—a slight accident, Tolliver. It's nothing to make a fuss about, but I want you to bring some hot-water bottles to Mrs. Ryeland's bedroom. Mix her a hot toddy, too, will you?"

Then he strode across the hall, not giving the manservant a chance to say anything in reply, mounting the stairs two at a time.

Rea could no longer think coherently.

Her head was going round and round as Burke carried her into the darkness of her bedroom and with a catlike assurance found her bed and laid her down upon it. Then he lit the lamps and stirred the logs in the fireplace, sending a shower of red sparks up the wide mouth of the chimney. Rea heard the dull clatter of the poker as Burke laid it back in the fender. Then he came back to her.

With an infinite gentleness, as though he tended a child, he stripped the scorched remains of her dress and her silken petticoats from her and put her into the dressing-gown which lay at the foot of the bed. He smiled down into her immense, tear-smudged eyes as he drew back the covers of the bed and laid her between their soft coolness. "How do you like me as a lady's maid?" he queried.

"You're—you're very good." She lay curled against her pillows like a spent kitten, aching and bruised from Jack Larchmont's pummelling hands, her mind still hung with lurid flame pictures. But all the same she attempted to return Burke's smile, watching him cross the room to answer Tolliver's discreet tap upon the door.

When Burke came back to the bedside, he was carrying hot-water bottles and a steaming silver tankard on a little tray that glittered as it caught the fluttering light of the oil-lamps. Burke set the tray down on the bed and carefully inserted the hot-water bottles. "Not too near your feet, are they?" he asked.

She shook her head. Already she was beginning to feel a little better—the raw, shocked ache of nerves and body soothed by the luxury of the big bed and the kindliness of Burke's ministrations.

"Going to sit up a minute or two for me? I want you to drink this toddy." He sat down on the side of the bed and drew her into the circle of his arms. He held the tankard while she sipped the hot, spicy contents.

His arm was warmly enveloping, his hand resting lightly over the soft tilt of her left breast. Rea sipped the toddy, knowing now, without surprise, that she loved this man. Loved him not with the half-grown heart of a child, but with the warm, enchanted, aching heart of a woman. Oh, that he could be so kind, when he thought that she—she and Jack Larchmont . . . A shudder of distress went through her body, a distress that was all the keener for the new delight she knew in having Burke's arm about her. She gazed down at his hand, gentle over her heart; saw the strength and beauty blended in that hand—and her heart turned over. She loved him, but she couldn't tell him, for Jack had saved her from the flames, and that, combined with the embrace Burke had witnessed under the dark cedars of Mallory Court, condemned her irretrievably; made her Jack's, in Burke's eyes, though every nerve in her screamed a protest that Jack should ever touch her again.

She loved, but her love was flowering in stony ground, for Burke only asked of her that she be a convincing mother for Peter. He asked no love of anyone for himself, breaking stones in a house of bondage for the girl he had loved too late!

She drew back from the tankard. "I—I don't want any more," she whispered.

"Sure?"

She nodded, and he set the tankard on one side. He laid her back against her pillows and was settling them more comfortably behind her head when he saw the weary, frightened tears break again in her eyes, spilling like great shining beads down her pale cheeks. "Why, you mustn't cry any more, Rea!" He bent over her in distress, pulling a handkerchief from his pocket and carefully dabbing at her tears. But still they came, and with something of alarm he gathered her back into his arms and rocked her, murmuring disjointedly: "Rea, you'll make yourself ill. Please stop crying! Please, child!"

But the storm had her in its grip and it was many minutes before her throat ceased to pulse with painful sobs. Then she lay very still in his arms, her lashes dark and wet on her cheeks, her soft hair dishevelled. "I—I'm sorry, Burke," she whispered at last, "but I had to cry. I couldn't help myself."

"Poor baby, I quite understand. You had a hellish fright." And then, as the full and terrible realization of what Rea had only narrowly escaped swept over Burke, his arms closed convulsively about her slight figure. He held her for a long silent moment, feeling the quick, nervous beat of her heart against him, his eyes darkly troubled. In a while her tear-smudged face drew away from his shoulder and she gave him a slight smile. "Thank you for being so kind, Burke," she murmured.

His answering smile was strained as he tweaked her fringe. "You do look a poor little scrap. Want to go to sleep now?"

She nodded and once again, very gently, he laid her back in the big bed, pulling the lace quilt to her chin. "Are you nice and warm?" he asked.

"Lovely," she said, and snuggled her face against her hand, languid now with tiredness as her lashes slowly spilled down upon her cheeks and her soft mouth slowly relaxed, emitting a little murmur—just like Peter, really, Burke thought, when he was drifting into sleep. Then, as the room grew still and the night sounds were muted beyond the casement, Rea went fast to sleep, her slenderness making almost no outline under the beautiful quilt, falling in rich scoops to the deep violet rugs at either side of the bed.

Burke studied Rea's small sleeping face with a curiosity abruptly touched with cynicism.

How could she look this innocent—touchingly innocent, with her gold-touched lashes soft upon her cheeks and her young mouth gathering colour back to its curves now that she slept away her trouble, when he had seen her, without innocence, in the arms of Jack Larchmont? Larchmont, an indiscriminate lecher, notorious for his affairs!

Burke drew a sigh that was both harsh and regretful as he rose from the bed. Oh well, Rea's life was her own. He had no real, lasting claim upon her. If she wanted Larchmont, who was he to say she couldn't have him?—Larchmont was, after all, the man who had dared the flaring maw of that bonfire for her.

Burke walked to the chest of drawers, turned out one of the lamps and left the other one just glimmering. Rea didn't like the shadowy loneliness of this room, he recalled.

CHAPTER FIFTEEN

TAB GRESHAM came down the stairs and crossed the hall to Burke's study. He tapped at the door and went in, his sandy brows lifting at the thick haze of cigarette smoke lying over the room. "Smoking yourself to death, old man?" he queried, closing the door and crossing the room to Burke, who was sprawled out in an armchair, one booted leg thrown over the other and a cigarette at a negligent angle in his mouth.

Burke's eyes smiled slightly. Then he said: "Well, how is she, Tab?"

"Tired, old man. And miserable. She says you haven't been to see her, that you sent Moira in to ask how she might be feeling." Tab put a finger against the scar upon his cheekbone. "I call that pretty cool of you, Burke, in the circumstances. That little girl came pretty close to death last night."

"What of our gallant hero, Larchmont?" Burke looked sardonic as he flicked ash into the fire. "How is he this morning?"

"He has some pretty nasty burns." Tab searched Burke's face with puzzled eyes. "What's biting you, may I ask?"

"Nothing!" The well-defined arches of Burke's eyebrows lifted in a studied surprise. "I'm quite as usual, Tab."

"Be damned to that!" Tab exploded. "You were acting mighty queer all last night, ignoring Rea, creeping off with Iris . . ."

"Doing what?" Burke's booted feet came to the floor with a thud.

"Don't deny it!" Tab's nondescript face was suddenly flushed with anger. "The two of you disappeared just before the firework display began."

"You were watching, eh—checking up?" Burke's eyes were half shut as they watched Tab, the glitter of them showing dangerously under the lowered lids. "But, Tab, I'm a married man now, I don't play Postman's Knock with other women any more, least of all with Iris." His lips curled upon a sarcastic smile. "It might astound you to hear this, Tab, but Iris leaves me quite cold."

"Then why . . .?" Tab stopped, abruptly embarrassed, the flush deepening in his cheeks.

"Why did she carry me off to the terrace?" Burke regarded the glowing end of his cigarette, his lips still wearing their thin smile. "She wanted to show me the Chinese lanterns."

Tab made a quick, annoyed, half embarrassed gesture with his hand. "I'm-I'm not one to pry, usually, you know that, Burke. It's just—I'd hate to see anything go wrong with your marriage. Rea—Rea's a fine girl."

"Is she?" Burke relaxed back into the wings of his big chair, crossing his legs again and watching a stream of wintry sun motes dancing in the haze of his cigarette smoke. "Now that, Tab, is what is called 'judging a book by its cover.' I made the same mistake."

"What do you mean?" Tab nervously ruffled his sandy hair as he watched Burke.

"I mean, Tab, that I mistook her for a child, with a child's innocent knowledge. I stole her, as I thought, from the cradle. I did it quite deliberately, and now I'm kicking because I've got to pay the usual price such folly demands—the price of shattered illusions." His eyelids lifted and he looked fully into Tab's perplexed face. "Rea, old friend, went and fell in love behind my back. I knew it could happen—yet I thought it a hundred years away from happening. She seemed," his big shoulders, clothed in a heavy maroon and white sweater, lifted on a shrug, "sort of enchanted, caught between the gauzy stages of turning from—from a bud into a rose." He drew hard on his cigarette, his black brows arched in a quizzing self-mockery. "I'm doomed, I think, to make mistakes about the people—no, the women I get involved with."

"Not Rea!" Tab spoke quickly, his tone decisive, without a shade of doubt or defensiveness in it. "Don't say of Rea that she'd ever betray your trust in her. She's utterly straight—I'd stake my life on it."

"But, Tab," Burke's smile was now more wintry than sarcastic, "I'm not talking about what might happen, I'm talking about what has happened."

"I—I can't believe—No, I won't believe wrong of Rea." Tab bent to Burke, his grey-blue eyes flashing. "Is it Larchmont? Are you thinking that he—"

"Larchmont and Rea," Burke said deliberately, "are in love. I don't know just how far it's gone, but, knowing Larchmont, I'd say pretty near the knuckle."

"Good God!" Tab straightened, staring at the windows through which dull sunshine was breaking and dying like dull waves upon the edge of a bleak beach. He thought of Larchmont's face as he had pounded the flames from the slight figure of Rea, an ivory mask of desperation, the eyes silently agonizing. Tab frowned. And this morning, when he had gone to the Larchmont farm to renew the dressings on Jack's hands, he had found him in a strangely subdued mood — for Jack Larchmont. No cynical comments, none of the caustic raillery he was notorious for. Tab had put his quietness down to the pain of his hands—but now—now Burke revealed a new reason for that quietness, a reason that bewildered and shocked Tab.

He swung round, staring hard at Burke. "Is Peter really your son, Burke?" he asked.

Burke's head jerked up. His eyes narrowed. "That's a peculiar question, Tab."

"I—I know." Again Tab ruffled his sandy hair, biting his lip in embarrassment. His reserved nature baulked at this invasion of another's privacy, yet, remembering Rea, lost and lonely in her big bed upstairs, forcing back tears as she said that Burke hadn't been to see her, he felt compelled to go on, to get to the bottom of this mystery. "I know, Burke. It's just—well, to put it quite frankly, certain aspects of your marriage are puzzling. I can't quite cotton to the fact that Rea has ever been in Peru."

"She hasn't," Burke returned crisply. He studied Tab a moment, then he tossed the stub of his cigarette into the fire. "Rea and I met just over two months ago. It was at Hastings—and I had a very strong reason for wanting a wife in a hurry."

"Peter?" Tab put in quietly.

Burke inclined his dark head. "Peter, as you say. Peter is Philip's son."

Tab wondered at his complete absence of surprise. He knew now that he had always thought that Burke's sudden and surprising yen for domesticity rang false, like an unsound coin. Marriage and babies—and Burke! Burke, who had always gone his own way, following the elusive will-o'-the-wisp of travel, and, if he ever paused by the wayside to enjoy the distraction of a pretty woman, pausing only long enough to ensure that the attraction didn't develop into anything deeper. Even Dani Larchmont, that wild, lovely thing, had not possessed a strong enough attraction for Burke to keep him from his wanderings.

Dani Larchmont! Tab's eyes suddenly flew open in a startled comprehension. Only a few months separated her death from Philip's—and why should a young creature like that die so suddenly? There was accident, of course, and fatal disease. There was also premature birth of a child.

Tab said, already knowing the answer: "Dani Larchmont was Peter's mother, wasn't she, Burke?"

Burke nodded. "Nasty, eh, Tab? I, at least, had the decency, if nothing else, to keep my lovemaking to a few kisses. Even so, those few kisses pushed her into Phil's arms. It was my fault, my fault, that he had his way." Burke's eyes were dark with self-condemnation, the muscles showing hard round his jaw. "I went away, Tab. I ran out on her because she said she loved me. Be damned to love, I thought, it put a man in chains. It binds him, demands that he give up his soul as well as his body. I wasn't having that—for all that she was so lovely and gay. I ran out on her, went to Peru, left her a letter saying that it was best our friendship ended, because I could never marry her. I cold-bloodedly told her, in that letter, to find herself someone who would give her marriage. I think," he drew a deep sigh, "I think she went quite deliberately to Phil after that—she went without scruple, and without scruple he took her. The rest you know. Phil died, Dani died, and I married Rea so that Peter could come here as my son. He is my son now, as a matter of fact. I legally adopted him."

Burke rose and walked past Tab to his desk. He took another cigarette, lit it. With his back to Tab, he said: "My marriage is an out-and-out fraud, Tab. I've no claim at all on Rea. When she comes to me and asks to be released, I shall release her."

"Because you think she loves Larchmont?"

"Because of just that," Burke retorted.

"But—but how can you be sure?"

Burke swung round, his dark face suddenly forbidding, the sapphire eyes blazing out of it. "I've seen them together. I've seen her in the fellow's arms. I'm not having old-maid delusions or anything, don't think it for a minute. I know what I'm talking about."

"Rea?" Tab shook a perplexed, unhappy head. "It seems hardly credible . . ."

"It's credible. I wasn't wearing dark glasses or blinkers. She was in Larchmont's arms and he was kissing her throat." Burke bit the words out. "I thought at first he was taking advantage of her, knowing Larchmont. I was going to give him a thrashing, but Rea went as white as paper and begged me, literally begged me, not to do it." Burke regarded the tip of his cigarette, a smile of deep cynicism breaking upon his lips. "The lady is my wife, so I obliged. I left her pretty little boy friend intact."

He glanced up at Tab, his mouth still wearing its smile of bitter cynicism. "You're wise to love Iris, I think. She's a pagan, and pagans never pretend to be angels. If you ever get her, Tab, you'll know exactly what you're getting; you'll never run up against a pile of shattered illusions, face first. Shattered illusions are nasty things—they cut, Tab. They cut like the very devil."

Tab had no answer to this. His own illusions concerning Rea had received a nasty jolt. No man, he knew, could look as Larchmont had looked last night, agonized with fear, unless the woman he saved meant the very breath of life to him. And a man didn't get that way about a woman just by looking at her—not Jack Larchmont's kind of man.

With a sigh, Tab turned to the door. "I'll be running along, old man, I've still got a few more calls to make.

I've told Rea to spend the day in bed. See that she does, will you?"

"She—is all right?"

"Perfectly. She just needs rest." Tab stood irresolutely by the door, one hand upon the doorknob. "Burke—has it ever occurred to you that Jack Larchmont might know that Peter belongs to Dani and Philip?"

Burke, after a momentary look of surprise, shook his head. "Polly Wilmot, Dani's aunt, assured me that Jim Larchmont was the only other person who knew about Peter. He couldn't be at the funeral—Vera Larchmont had that stroke and he didn't dare leave her, as you know—but directly he was able to leave her he hurried to Hastings to see Polly Wilmot, where, naturally, he found out about Peter. But he didn't dare take the boy home with him. He knew Vera would never have survived the double shock of learning that her beloved Dani had died having Philip Ryeland's child." Burke's face twisted into a sardonic grimace. "Vera has always entertained rather high-flown ideas about the blue-blooded chivalry of the Ryelands."

"All the same," Tab fiddled nervously with the study doorknob, "I still think Jack could have found out."

"Not possible!" Burke broke in curtly. "He wasn't living at home at the time of Dani's death, you know that. He was up in Ireland, helping to train greyhounds, or some such business. He didn't come back to Somerset until weeks after Dani's burial, when he got thrown out of his job in Ireland—where you can bet he was up to something shady." Burke frowned blackly. "No, Tab, Jack doesn't know about Peter. If he'd known, he'd have used that knowledge; he's not the sort to baulk at blackmail, believe me."

"Nice character!" Tab's face was gloomy. "Yet you assert that Rea—"

"Oh, lord, don't let's get back to that!" Burke spoke with an abrupt weariness. "Larchmont's bad—but he's what Rea wants. Maybe—maybe she'll make a better man of him. He dared, last night, what very few men would dare, after all."

"That's true." Tab thought of the ugly, painful burns Jack now bore upon his hands and forearms for Rea, and he knew himself bewildered and out of his depth. Love—what was love? His own love for Iris had seemed real enough, strong enough, to him, yet it had burned right out in the bonfire at Mallory Court last night, even as Jack Larchmont's had seemed to come glowingly alive.

Burned out . . . gone out . . . and all he seemed able to feel for her now was an empty, disgusted sort of pity; an awareness that he had always secretly known that she'd finally do something he could never, never forgive. Among the ashes there merely burned a remnant of relief that Burke had no knowledge that it was Iris who had caused Rea's accident. Burke wouldn't spare Iris, as he, Tab, must spare her for the sake of what he had once felt . . .

Then, with a rather defeated sigh, Tab pulled open the study door and plunged from Burke's sight, calling out a hasty goodbye.

Rea lay gazing up at the draped tester of her bed, her eyes too big in her face and shadowed by a fear that had no relation to last night's fear.

The bonfire at Mallory Court last night had been a nightmare, flaring into her life and then out again. Even the vitality it had taken from her had been restored to her in the long sleep which had followed her tears in Burke's arms.

This fear was real as the daylight beyond her bedroom casements, and as fast as her tormented mind ran from it, it caught up with her again.

"You'd best go, miss," Betty had said. "That Jack, he says he'll come up to the house if you don't go. He says he'll wait in the wood, miss, all afternoon . . ."

All afternoon? And if she didn't go, he would come up to the house!

Rea's head turned restlessly on her rumpled pillows. How could she go? It was Sunday, and Burke was in the house. Burke! He hadn't been in to see her. He had sent Moira, instead, to ask how she might be feeling, much as Jack had sent Betty, but Jack had said: "Tell her I *want* to see her. Tell her I *must* see her."

Rea bit her lip, her eyes moving to the bedroom casements as they rattled in a testy wind, much as though a hand shook them and a voice, with an insolent caress in it, said outside them: "I'm here, Rea. I came."

Each time the stable clock struck the quarter-hours, the half-hours, then the hours, the wind carried the chimes to Rea, increasing her restlessness and her fear. Soon, soon, the afternoon would have worn away . . .

Then, quite suddenly, she grew very still in her big bed. That was Rebel, surely, below in the stable-yard? Yes, it was Rebel! Rea lifted herself on her elbow, and plain, now, came those excited whinnyings Rebel always made when Burke was mounting him. Rea's hand slowly took hold of the lace quilt covering her bed, her fingers clenching the lace, her heart feeling as though it beat in every part of her. Rebel's hooves chattered on the kidney stones and Rea knew that Burke was now in the saddle, tall and breeched, his eyes very blue as he trotted Rebel round the side of the house, into the wind that came crying down off the Mendips. The wind brought the trot-trot of Rebel's hooves to Rea, then, as the big horse was urged into a canter, the sounds soon died right away—and Rea was scrambling from her bed.

She hurried into her clothes and combed her hair with a hand that shook. Five minutes later she had slipped from the house and was running across the meadow.

Rea went into the wood and the old, ghostly rustlings followed her and the big trees seemed to watch her. She shivered and drew the collar of her coat up about her throat, and under her fingers there was the sudden slender feel of the chain holding Burke's cameo. Her fingers touched and suddenly clung, as though to a lifeline . . .

"So you came?" said a quiet voice behind her.

She spun round. She stared up into Jack Larchmont's eyes, the cameo dropping from her suddenly nerveless hand, back into the pale hollow of her throat.

"You're pale, little Rea," Jack murmured. "Did you sleep and forget the flames? I hope you did."

"I—I'm all right." Her gaze fell to his heavily bandaged hands and her brow contracted, as though at a dart of pain. "I—I hope your hands don't pain you too much." Her eyes lifted again to his face, full of a sudden compassion. "Why—why did you do it? Why? Getting so hurt . . ."

"You know why." Suddenly the slanting eyes burned as they watched her and a vivid flush dyed Rea's throat, mounting all the way to her forehead. She half turned from him, throwing out an appealing hand. "Don't! Please!"

"Why, because you still hate me?"

She shook her head quickly. "No—no, I don't hate you. You saved my life. I can't hate you."

"Can you love me?" The question came with great deliberateness, and the slanting eyes narrowed as he took a sudden step close to her. "Won't you love me?"

"I—I can't!" She turned all the way from him, leaning the pounding ache of her forehead against the rough lichen of a big oak. She was shaking, as though with a fever. "I can't! I love Burke. He's all the world to me."

"And what are you to him? The little unquestioning cog in his big wheel of deception—nothing more. When it suits him to throw you aside he'll do it. He only lives to suit himself, haven't you learned that yet? Oh, he's very pleasant and charming, quite the gallant, but don't be fooled, Rea. His charm is all on his tongue. He hasn't got a heart to feel with, like other people. I hold him directly responsible for my sister's death. She was as pretty as paint, crowds of men after her, but he charmed her with that damn tongue of his, turned her silly with love for him, then ran out on her. She didn't care after that. Didn't care who she went to. And you say you love him! How can you love him?"

"He—he's always been kind to me." A lump rose in Rea's throat as she recalled the many times Burke had comforted her with a smile, with reassuring words in that deep, pleasant voice of his. "He once spoke to me about your sister, about how lovely she was. He didn't mean to break her life—he didn't do it maliciously."

"Don't give me that!" Jack exclaimed. "He's rich and spoiled, and Dani was just another toy he'd grown tired of. He dropped her and strode off and that was that."

"Not quite!" In sudden passion Rea turned to Jack, her hazel eyes blazing out of her pale face. "Burke has ensured that one day King's Beeches and everything pertaining to it becomes the property of your sister's child. It's immaterial to him that if ever he should have a child of his own, that child will take second place to Peter."

"And who will give him that child—you?" Jack demanded. Then he gave a harsh, insolent laugh. "Don't tell me he's your lover! You've never had a lover!"

"No," Rea shook her head, her gaze falling away from the insolence burning in Jack's eyes. "No, I've never had a lover."

"But you will have one, Rea." His voice suddenly vibrated with feeling, and insolence was banished from his eyes, replaced by a warm, lambent glow. "You'll come to me in the beginning because you must, but you'll stay in the end because you can't help yourself. You'll catch fire from my love, Rea, but I'll not put those flames out."

"Oh, don't! I won't listen to you!" Rea put her hands over her ears, her face anguished. "I could never love you—never—never—never!"

"Never can end in a night, Rea." Jack gave a soft little laugh. "In a night, you innocent baby. Now, when do I come up to King's Beeches to see that husband of yours? Tonight? The sooner we talk divorce, the better, I think."

"Divorce!" Rea looked at him as though he had gone mad. "What are you talking about?"

"Your divorce, honey." Jack's smile was indulgent. "Naturally you must get divorced. I want to marry you. I want you for always. What else did you think I wanted?"

Rea stared at him, searching his dark, gipsy face with bewildered eyes. Marriage? With this man? Her heart turned cold inside her. Her mind reeled. The wild possession of her heart and her body, which he envisaged, which he called love, seemed to open a pit of horror in front of her eyes. "You're mad!" she gasped. "I—I'd rather be dead than married to you!"

Jack's dark brows rose in two taunting peaks above his dark eyes. "You're hardly complimentary, little Rea, but I was never a man to appreciate an easy conquest—

the apples that don't fall into the grass are always the tastiest." He glanced down at his bandaged hands, a rueful smile curving his lips. "Tell me, though, what makes love so repugnant to you? Don't you believe that it is love?"

"I—I believe that you think it is," Rea cried back. "But love—love isn't greedy and demanding. It doesn't devour." She faced him in a trembling defiance, her face a small colourless triangle, the violet smudges under her eyes grown suddenly deeper. "Love is wanting to give, not to take."

"You'd know, of course," he sneered, "besotted with love for Ryeland as you are! Well, you're going to forget all that! You're going to come with me!"

"No! I—I can't—I can't!" She backed from him, her hands held out beseechingly. "Please, Jack . . ."

"Please, Jack!" he mocked. He moved towards her, excited by the white appeal of her face, the dark, fear-drowned hazel of her eyes. "Damn these hands!" he said. "I want to kiss you, Rea! I want you!"

"No! No!" She turned then, ran wildly from him, careering through the trees, blundering over the stretched roots of them, crying out as the lower branches plucked at her hair. When she reached the meadow gate she was sobbing dryly with fear, her legs barely supporting her over the white bars. She stumbled across the meadow, wanting only to get to the house, to get to the quiet sanctuary of her room. She would be safe there—Jack couldn't touch her there . . . She glanced wildly back over her shoulder, but he hadn't followed her. She gasped with relief—and even as she knew relief—as she reached the stable-yard and would have darted across the kidney-stones into the house, Rebel trotted round the side of the house and Rea was looking up at Burke.

Her pounding heart turned all the way over as he swung from Rebel's saddle and reached out a hand, pulling her towards him. His face was harsh in the rapidly fading daylight, and in the long seconds before he spoke, Rea listened to the dismal mewing of a few birds in the grey sky overhead and it seemed to her that their plaintive noise was exactly the right accompaniment to this moment, for her heart, too, felt as though it mewed and flapped sad wings in a winter sky.

"I know where you've been, of course," Burke said crisply. "You've been to see Larchmont!" His fingers suddenly bit into her shoulder and a spasm of intense anger flared his decisive nostrils. "It must have been sheer agony for you, my dear, having to control your eagerness to get to him until I was out of the house." Abruptly, then, he released her shoulder and gave her a push towards the house. "Go to my study," he said curtly. "We'll talk there."

Drearily she obeyed him, and when he came to the study, about ten minutes later, she was crouched down in front of the log fire, staring into the blaze, the blaze lighting the side of her hair to a soft gold and dancing its shadows across her thin, pale cheek.

Burke stood with his back to the door, his eyes like blue stones as they moved over her. Her air of waiting humility, the childlike attitude she had assumed in front of the fire, seemed to drop him into an even deeper scorn. When he began to speak his voice was deadly still, each word an arrow of ice, aimed with the bitter intent to reveal not only his scorn for her, but his scorn for himself, because he had let her air of innocence fool him.

"I'll tell you here and now, Rea," he said, "that I'll not tolerate a wife who shares my roof and conducts a love affair with an abysmal creature like Larchmont every time I'm out of the house for a few hours. If you're so eaten up with him that you can't keep away from him, then I think it best you go to him altogether." And as Rea's eyes slowly drew away from the hypnotic flare of the apple logs and settled on the stone mask of his face, he said, quite impersonally now: "You are quite at liberty to go to him, Rea. Go now. That foolish bargain of ours is cancelled—I release you from it. You don't have to snatch at chance moments to meet your pretty little lover any more, you're free as air to go to him for good—and I'd prefer it if you went tonight."

With these words he walked across to the desk, stood with his back to her as he took and lit a cigarette. He heard her quiet steps move to the door, heard the door open and then close—and as it closed, his big shoulders slumped. Harsh anger and wounded pride drained out of him and all that was left was the memory of how she had looked last night, white and fragile in the big fourposter, leaning without weight in the circle of his arm. He lifted his cigarette and drew deeply upon it. So this—this was what a lonely, one-sided love did to one, tore the heart wide open and left it naked and hurt and humiliated? Behind him a log broke open in the fireplace, and the small, sharp noise it made touched the raw exposure of his nerves and he swung round with a startled grimace. The room was very empty now, invaded by dusk and the sudden patter of rain on the windows. A small groan broke from him and he knew that in this moment he paid fully for Dani Larchmont's lonely, one-sided love.

CHAPTER SIXTEEN

DINNER came to an end and Burke curtly declined to join his grandfather in a game of cards.

The old man rose from the table, straightening his velvet dinner-jacket and watching Burke with sharp eyes. When Rea had not appeared for dinner he had enquired of her whereabouts, naturally, and though immediate satisfaction had lit up in him to hear his grandson dispassionately announce that she had left King's Beeches, probably for good, that satisfaction had slowly turned rather sour in him as dinner progressed. Whatever had induced her departure from the house—and Burke had not enlightened him on that point—one thing was very clear to Mr. Ryeland, her departure was neither welcomed nor wanted by Burke. Dash it, the boy looked ill—actually looked ill!

"Look here, boy, you're not going to brood after that little chit, are you?" The stiff white brows worked rapidly, as they always did when the old man was disturbed. "In my opinion, you're well rid of her!"

"Am I?" Burke's eyes held a sudden dangerous glint as they met his grandfather's.

"Certainly you are, my boy. I can't think what you ever saw in her. Her conversational powers were nil."

"Perhaps it wasn't her conversational powers I admired," Burke curtly rejoined, and his grandfather saw his hands slowly clench at his sides until the knuckles gleamed white under the brown skin. The old man cleared his throat, almost embarrassedly. "You've still got the boy," he remarked, and as he mentioned the child whom he thought to be Rea's, he was reminded of the many times he had come upon her with that chuckling, blue-eyed child in her arms. Burke's boy, touching the pale satin of Rea's hair with plump fingers; nuzzling her throat with a face adorned with rusk crumbs . . .

"Dash it, Burke, if you want the girl, why have you let her go?" he demanded.

"Because my wants don't happen to coincide with hers," Burke retorted.

Mr. Ryeland received this with a snort of disgust. "What's the matter with you, boy—gone soft in the head? Her wants not coincide with yours! Go after her, give her a good old-fashioned shaking, bring her to heel!" The old hands went hard into the pockets of the velvet dinner-jacket and the fading blue eyes stared across the table into Burke's brooding blue eyes. "She loves that child upstairs. Won't she come back for him?"

Burke didn't answer. He turned aside to light a cigarette from a lighter on the sideboard and the action was jerky, fumbling, without the lithe ease of movement that usually characterized him, in and out of the saddle; sitting or standing. He took a deep lungful of cigarette smoke, then he walked to the dining-room door and jerked it open. "Rea won't come back," he said. "There's nothing here she wants." He turned his head briefly and gave his grandfather a cynical smile. "But you should be feeling pleased, sir—you've got what you wanted."

He stepped out into the hall with these words and was about to cross to his study when Tolliver's voice arrested him. "Yes, Tolliver?" He swung round, eyeing the butler with impatience.

"Mr. Jack Larchmont is here, sir," Tolliver said. "I've shown him into the library."

"Jack Larchmont!" Quick colour ran up under the brown skin of Burke's face and Tolliver's eyes opened wide in his smooth, expressionless face as the thumb and forefinger of Burke's right hand slowly buckled the cigarette he held. Then he turned sharply on his heel and crossed to the library with long strides.

Jack lounged, with bandaged hands, against the back of the big couch in the library, watching the door with insolent eyes.

"Good evening, Ryeland!" he said.

Burke banged the door shut behind him and crossed the room to Jack, towering above him. "What are you doing here?" he demanded.

"I've come to ask you to release Rea," Jack drawled.

Burke's nostrils flared, and for seconds on end his

impulse to take hold of Jack by the scruff of his neck and soundly shake him was barely held in check. He said, at last, in a low, savage voice: "I told Rea I'd release her. She didn't have to send you up here."

"Send me?" One of Jack's slender black brows lifted enquiringly. "Rea didn't send me, old man. What are you talking about?"

"Well, she's at your place, isn't she? Naturally I assumed—"

"At my place—at the farmhouse?" Jack suddenly straightened from his lounging position and his glance sharpened as it moved over Burke's face. "Look here, Ryeland, what are you talking about? Rea isn't at my place."

"She has to be!" The decisive bones of Burke's face seemed suddenly more pronounced. "I tell you she has to be! I told her she was free to go to you."

"Did you now?" Jack's eyes had grown thoughtfully narrow. "When was this, may I ask?"

"About two and a half hours ago." Suddenly Burke's control broke and he reached out and closed a hard, angry hand upon Jack's shoulder. He jerked Jack towards him and shook him roughly, disregarding his heavily bandaged hands. "Don't play with me, Larchmont," he ground out. "I know full well Rea is at your place—where else could she go?"

"That's the question." Jack, unable to use his hands to fight free of Burke's grasp, bore the indignity with a rueful smile. "Where could she go, Ryeland? Where did she go, for I swear to you she isn't at the farmhouse."

Burke stared down at him, searching the insolent, handsome face with fierce eyes. "I'm in no mood to be played with, Larchmont. If you're lying to me—"

"I'm many things, Ryeland," Jack shot back, "but I'm no liar. I haven't a notion where Rea is—if she isn't here."

"She—she isn't here." Burke gave a sudden groan and released Jack. "I told her to go, to get out. I—I thought, naturally, she'd run to you—you're her lover."

"Am I?" Jack watched Burke with curious eyes. "Is that what you really think?"

"I've seen you making love to her!"

"Ah, yes, under the cedars at Iris Mallory's birthday dance." Jack's drawl had returned, with its old undercurrent of careless insolence. "You wanted to break my neck, didn't you? You would have broken it, doubtless, if Rea hadn't leapt into the breach. Rea has a gentle heart. I believe she'd walk right round a crawling beetle rather than cause it a moment's pain by treading on it." Jack glanced down at his bandaged hands and there came back to him that despairing cry of Rea's in the wood that afternoon; the cry that begged him to understand even as she had to say: "I can't, I can't."

But he had to have her!

Jack glanced up again at Burke, and hate shocked through him like the touch of sudden lightning as his eyes rested upon that strong, tawny face, stripped now of its pride and its self-containment, true, but still the face that had beguiled Dani into love and then coolly turned aside from that love. "So you've had a bust-up with Rea and thrown her out of the old ancestral home, eh?" Jack, white with hate, threw out a bandaged hand towards the windows, where rain drummed loudly behind the damask curtains. "I must say you've chosen a delightful night for it, Ryeland! Hear that rain? Rea's out in it—"

"God, don't you think I know that!" Burke strode to the nearest window. He jerked aside the curtain and frowned out upon the rain-swept night. A high wind howled down from the Mendips and even the powerful beeches lowered their heads before it, their branches whipping sharply, angrily together. "I—I felt certain she'd come to you, Larchmont." Burke swung round from the window and Jack saw the sudden pinched look about his nostrils, the pain and bewilderment in the blue eyes that usually regarded everyone and everything with such a self-assured coolness. "Have I misjudged Rea?" Burke moved from the windows and began to come across the carpet to Jack once more. "I've got to know, Larchmont!" Now he stood over Jack. "I've got to know what you mean to Rea."

"But you know, old man." Jack's thin lips barely moved to make these five words, but the world of meaning he managed to instil into them re-woke Burke to a flash of that intolerable jealousy he had known earlier on in the evening when he had ordered Rea to leave King's Beeches; to go to Larchmont. Jealousy flared raw and sharp along his veins, fed by that insistent picture of Rea in this man's embrace.

"Damn it all, Larchmont," he burst out, "you're not good enough for her! She's sweet and untried and you've dazzled her—"

"I've dazzled her!" Jack stared up into Burke's eyes, his own eyes grown as suddenly hard and glinting as black agate—and neither man knew that in that moment the library door opened and Burke's grandfather stood tall and thin in the aperture. "You'd know all about dazzling a girl, wouldn't you, Ryeland?" Jack cried out. "You practised plenty on my poor sap of a sister—and then ran out on her! She wasn't good enough for you, was she? Not good enough to mingle her peasant blood with your wonderful Ryeland blood! But Philip didn't like that, did he? Lord, no, Philip didn't hesitate to cash in on Dani's susceptibility to you damn Ryelands! That kid Peter belongs to Dani and Philip—"

Then, with a sharp intake of breath, Jack swung to the sound of a groan by the library door. Burke did the same, a grimace of quick distress crossing his face as he saw his grandfather. Damn Larchmont to hell—so he *had* known about Peter!

"That isn't true! That's a vile blasphemy against my boy—my Philip!" The old man stepped out from the shadows by the door and the sudden full play of overhead light on his face revealed the putty colour of the taut skin over his hawk nose and high cheekbones. He came steadily towards Jack, raising his fist and shaking it. "I'll have you run off King's Beeches for what you've just said, Larchmont!"

"It happens to be true!" Jack retorted, that insolent courage of his not deserting him as Burke's grandfather drew closer; a taunting smile springing upon his lips as the bony fist, shaking with anger, struck at his smile—struck twice, the sounds loud and painful in the room.

"There's no need for that, sir!" With one decisive stride Burke was behind his grandfather and holding his high, thin shoulders with restraining hands. "Larchmont's talking rot, there's no need for you to take any notice of him—"

"To hell with that!" Jack's eye burned deeply above the ugly marks Mr. Ryeland had made upon his mouth. "I'm thinking it's about time some of this stiff-necked pride was let out of this house and some truth let in." The slanting, burning eyes were fixed upon the grey proud face confronting him. "That kid Peter doesn't belong to Burke. He's your precious Philip's kid—by my sister."

"Shut up, damn you!" Burke ordered.

"By—my—sister!" Jack repeated, slowly, ignoring Burke. "By—my—sister! Little Dani Larchmont! Little farm-girl Dani Larchmont! And do you want to know something else—something else that'll scorch that infuriating Ryeland pride of yours? Philip married my sister! Yeah—he married her! And he was so damned uncertain of that so-called love of yours for him that he begged Dani to keep the marriage a secret. He knew you'd throw him out of King's Beeches if you found out he was human enough to want love. He knew you wouldn't let him have King's Beeches and love. He knew he had to give body and soul to this damn house—"

"Are you speaking the truth, Larchmont?" Burke broke in, his eyes gone a brilliant, eager blue as he watched Jack's face. "Dani's aunt said nothing about a marriage between Dani and Phil—"

"She didn't know." Jack shrugged his shoulders. "Aunt Polly Wilmot likes to gossip, so Dani let her think—well, what she did think. I only found out about the marriage because I spent a few days at Dani's flat in London—I was down from Ireland to see about selling dogs. Three of the brutes died and I was short of cash." Jack's mouth twisted into his characteristic half bitter, half insolent smile. "I went through the drawers of Dani's dressing-table, hoping she might have a quid or two tucked away among her undies. I found her marriage certificate instead. When I confronted her with it that evening, when she got back from the theatre, she got a bit hysterical. She'd found out by then that she didn't really want Philip—that she wanted you—still wanted you!" Jack stared hatefully into Burke's eyes. "D'you know what she did, then? She snatched her marriage lines out of my hand and threw them in the fire. As they flared up and went to ashes, she said: 'Phil needn't worry—I'm happy to keep this miserable little marriage a secret!' "

"And a secret it remained," Burke said quietly. Under his hands his grandfather's shoulders were trembling hard, and Burke didn't have to look at the elderly face to know that the blow he had just been dealt was agonizing him.

"Look, sir," Burke spoke in a low, passionate tone, "don't go holding this against Phil. Dani Larchmont was an extremely lovely girl and Phil was young enough to be enchanted by her loveliness. I was myself—"

"You!" With a jerk of his shoulders Mr. Ryeland pulled free of Burke's hands. He flung round to face him. "You're more despicable than Philip and this Larchmont fellow put together—playing your damn games with me! Why couldn't you have told me that the child belonged to Philip?"

"I didn't dare!" Burke returned flatly. "It seemed only right to me that Peter come home here to King's Beeches, but I knew he'd stand very little chance of doing so if you knew Dani Larchmont had borne him to Phil—out of wedlock, as I thought. God knows why you had to hate that girl!"

"God knows why you had to love her!" His grandfather spat back at him. "Wild, dancing, gipsy creature!"

"I—love Dani?" Burke stepped back sharply from this accusation. "I never loved Dani!"

"You took the girl about! D'you think no one knew that down here? The girl's mother bragged right and left about her precious daughter's courtship."

"I never loved Dani!" A nerve was pulsing hard in Burke's jaw as he stared down at his grandfather. "I admired her beauty, valued her friendship, but I never wanted more than friendship from her. When I saw that she was giving me more, I—I ended our association. The only excuse I can offer is that I thought her too beautiful and popular to feel the loss of one boy friend for very long—my cynicism, you see, just couldn't be dented in those days by any real belief in the substance of—love." Burke half shrugged his wide shoulders, his eyes gone dark blue as his self-contempt clouded them. "I've learned since that the strongest wall of cynicism can fall, and don't think I haven't been punished for giving Dani stones to eat!"

For a long moment Burke stared at the library windows, listening to the rain and the raw moan of the lonely winds he had thrust Rea out in . . .

His eyes came back to his grandfather's face and he went on: "I couldn't see Dani's boy thrust into an orphanage, and I thought it a wonderful stroke of luck when I met Rea—there's an air of innocence about Rea that could make of any deception a reality, and I knew you'd be deceived by it, that you'd accept Peter without question when you saw him in—in Rea's arms."

"Clever of you!" Mr. Ryeland's face was a livid mask above the claret of his dinner-jacket. "You've always thought yourself mighty clever, haven't you—above being a mere farmer? Well," the old man drew his thin, trembling body up very straight, the pinched whiteness about his nostrils sharpening and making suddenly cruel the hawk-like fashioning of his nose, "well, this place doesn't need you. I can employ a land-agent to do what you do, give service without love. King's Beeches doesn't need you—just as that girl doesn't need you—nor I!" With a swift, contemptuous gesture, Mr. Ryeland snapped his fingers in Burke's face. "Nor I!"

"What of the boy?" Burke stared hard into his grandfather's glacial eyes. "The law has now made me his father. What if I take him away? What will there be left for you, apart from this house, this mere mass of bricks and mortar? Much as you love this house, can you hold it in your arms and hear it laugh and see it grow from day to day? Can you say with real honesty that you hate Peter?"

"I—I—" Old Mr. Ryeland drew back both physically and mentally from this question. "I—he's Philip's son—"

"Yes, he's Philip's son," Burke agreed quietly. "Can you hate him—is it in you to hate him, to thrust him to one side, when you know that Phil's blood flows in him and that Phil's love for King's Beeches has probably been bequeathed to him? Dare you hate him and thereby persecute yourself to loneliness?"

"Be quiet!" The harsh command rang out loudly in the library, rang out almost with hysteria above the drumming of rain upon the windows, the deep beat of the pendulum clock upon the wall, the hiss of the bright burning logs in the fireplace . . .

"Dare you?" Burke insisted. "Dare you shut Peter, along with me, outside that—that citadel of Ryeland pride you dwell in? If that's to be the way of it, I'll take the boy away. I'll take him tonight—"

Faded blue eyes, full of pain and anger, warred with the sapphire eyes of Burke . . . The Ryeland eyes, that had been Philip's . . .

"No!" The word broke sharply in the room. "No!" The sharp-boned shoulders slowly lost some of their tautness and the anger began to drain out of the hawk face. "We're fools, the pair of us, shouting at one another. The boy stays here, of course he does." The white brows flickered, the faded blue eyes sharply examined Burke's face. "You both stay—of course you do. I—I spoke in anger a moment ago. Anger that you couldn't have told me the truth, for though the things I've learned tonight have hurt me, I can't lose that little lad upstairs."

"Dani was his mother," Burke reminded him crisply. "If you hadn't taken it into your head to dislike her because she was lovely in a wild, strange way, and because she danced for her living, none of the bitter words we've had to speak tonight would ever have been spoken and Phil wouldn't have thought it wise instead of a folly to keep his marriage a secret. If you can accept Dani, at last, then Peter and I will stay. I don't want to hurt you more than you have been hurt."

"I think you would kill me, boy, if you took—if you took the little lad away. I'm not such a man of stone." The old eyes stared into Burke's eyes and now they were made humble by regret. "I'm not, y'know. I—God help me—I don't want to spend the few months I've got left in loneliness, though I deserve it—though I deserve it!" One of the old hands came forward and touched Burke's sleeve. "Dash it, this is your home. You inherit—and a provision can always be made in your will about the boy following you, if you want it that way."

"My home?" Burke's smile was wry. "Perhaps it might have become that—if I could have kept Rea."

"No longer a house bondage, eh, if you could have kept that pale-haired chit?" The old eyes swept over Burke's face with sudden shrewdness. "But, my boy, the marriage was a farce altogether, wasn't it?"

"Yes."

"You damn young fool, no wonder she's left you! French blood in your veins, too."

Burke received this with wryly lifted brows. Jack Larchmont burst out laughing.

At once Mr. Ryeland swung round upon him, harsh anger back in his face. "Get out of my house, Larchmont!" he ordered. "Walk out, now, before I have my dogs chase you out."

"Oh, I'm going, don't you fret yourself." Still laughing a little, Jack walked to the open door, but at the door he turned a moment. He said to Burke: "You were mighty surprised that I knew about Dani and Philip, weren't you, Ryeland?"

"Naturally." Burke's face was contemptuous. "I should have thought you'd have resorted to blackmail. What was holding you back? Peter's story was a real plum for you—why did you hesitate to pluck it?"

"Perhaps I didn't hesitate!" Jack retorted, looking at once insolent and enigmatic. Then he went from the library, leaving the door wide open behind him.

Burke stood like a stone man, watching Tolliver in the hall with Jack, helping him on with his shabby raincoat. Then Tolliver walked with Jack to the front door and a moment later it clapped shut on Jack's departure.

"Perhaps I didn't hesitate!" The words beat in Burke's brain, and he was seeing Rea's face again, as it had looked that afternoon—white, fearful, tormented! God, had he made a mistake about the white fear her face had worn? He had thought it borne there because he had caught her stealing back from her meeting with Jack . . .

"Perhaps I didn't hesitate!"

Then Burke started violently as a hand touched his shoulder. He swung round, staring at his grandfather. "Boy," Mr. Ryeland said, "where's the girl gone, back to London?" He shook Burke's shoulder impatiently. "If that's it, go after her! The earliest train she can catch is the eight-forty-five."

"I—" Burke's blue eyes were suddenly boyishly diffident. "I don't think she loves me, sir. I told her to go, you see, and she went. I think she was glad to run from all the lies . . . How Rea hated all those lies! She said, right at the beginning of things, that I should tell you the truth—or what I thought of as the truth at the time. God, does there ever come a time when we human creatures stop making mistakes? The mistakes I've made! How do I ever remedy them?"

"Go to the station." Burke's grandfather gave him a push. "If you don't, boy, you may be making the biggest mistake you ever made!"

CHAPTER SEVENTEEN

THAT old man, Jack thought, trudging in the rain down the drive of King's Beeches. That old man, talking as though God did recompense for losses! Jack held his face to the rain and he was near the gates when Burke's grey car screeched to a halt beside him. Burke flung open the car door to yell at him: "Jump in! I'll drop you off at the farmhouse."

"No, thanks," Jack said.

"But it's on my way—"

"To the railway station?" Jack's smile was totally without humour. "And you feel you can be generous, eh, to a blackmailer?"

"Quite truthfully, Larchmont," Burke said, "I'd like to wring your neck."

"And then you remember that last night I saved Rea's life and once again you feel you can be generous." The reflections from the headlights lit Jack's thin, handsome face, splashed with rain and cynical with self-mockery. "Sir Galahad," he drawled, "you shouldn't be streaking to your knightly errand in that very modern racer. You should be sitting high and wide on a white charger." His taunting grin came and went. "I thought of the railway station a good half hour ago—but then I had inside information, didn't I?"

"You're a swine!" Burke retorted succinctly. Then he slammed shut the door of the car and shot forward into the night.

It took Burke twenty minutes to reach the railway station, and when he strode into the waiting-room, very wet and very angry with the night and himself and the whole wretched web of intrigue he had involved Rea in, he was looking strangely unlike himself. He stared round the waiting-room, his eyes a blind, shocked blue, for the room held only a fume-belching oil-stove and a snore-racked farmer in muddied leggings and boots. There was no Rea, with her fringe tumbling above her wide eyes. No Rea—

He swung sharply on his heel and made for the ticket office, banging impatiently on the window.

The window shot up and the ticket man eyed Burke irritably from behind rimless spectacles. "What's all the noise?" he demanded. He wasn't a Somerset man and the aggression of the town voice seemed to increase for Burke his feeling of unrest. "Where d'you want to go?"

"Look," Burke swept the raindrops from his face as he peered through the window, "I thought the London train didn't get in till eight-forty-five?"

"Nor it don't." The ticket man glanced round at the clock on the wall of his office. "You've got another ten minutes. Want a ticket?"

"No." Burke shook his head. "The fact of the matter is, I thought a young lady might be waiting for the train. Has a young lady been in to buy a ticket?" His wild blue eyes searched the man's face. "Please—it's rather important."

"Well, now," the ticket man rubbed the side of his nose and eyed Burke's desperation of expression with something of suspicion, "there was a young gel in here —young, thin thing, all eyes—"

"That's her—that's Rea!" Burke's eyes lit up and his cry of relief rang round the dim, hollow, damp-smelling station. His hands clasped the sill of the ticket-office window and he seemed ready to shake the sill from its bearings. "How long ago was this—why didn't she wait?" he demanded.

"Now, now, there's no need to get so rattled," retorted the ticket man testily, a slight sneer to his lip that anything male could display so much excitement over that skinny half-drowned creature who had wandered into the station around about seven o'clock and bought a ticket for London. "It's like this, mister. Young Doctor Gresham turned up 'ere about an hour ago, came to collect a parcel he's been expecting, new microscope or something, and I happened to mention this 'ere gel to him, for she looked kind of queer and ill to me when she bought 'er ticket. So he goes off to the waiting-room, like, just to take a look at 'er, and the next thing I know—he's carting 'er out of 'ere. And that, mister, was an hour ago."

"Thanks! Thanks a million!"

"That's all right—" The words trailed off, for Burke's tall, black-clad figure was gone, the loud clap-clap-clap of the station doors echoing out behind him, testifying to the whirlwind manner in which he had passed through them.

Burke swung his car out of the station yard and made rapidly for Tab's house, the other side of the village. He was there in under seven minutes and it was Mrs. Jarrett, Tab's housekeeper, who answered the door to his imperative rat-tat.

"The doctor isn't in, dearie, he's had to go over t'road to birth the smithy's wife's twins." She pulled the door open a little wider and as the hall light showed her the doctor's caller with more clearness, her kindly, elderly mouth emitted an 'ooh' of startled surprise. "You, sir!" she gasped.

"Mrs. Jarret," Burke's voice held a tremor, his eyes a plea, "is my wife here?"

There was an old-fashioned horsehair sofa in Tab's rather old-fashioned parlour, and Rea was curled up on this, gazing into the fire. She had not yet had a real chance to talk to Tab, for immediately on their arrival here from the station, Mrs. Jarret had informed Tab that he was urgently wanted over at the blacksmith's, where the blacksmith's wife was on the verge of giving birth to twins. Tab had had to go, but he had exacted a promise from Rea that she would stay in the house, in the warm, until they had talked. And Rea, wearied and damp, and overwhelmingly comforted by Tab's concern for her, had agreed. In any case, running away to London wouldn't really have helped matters—and she knew tiredly that in the end she wouldn't have boarded the train.

With a little moan she turned her face into the leather of the sofa. What was she going to do about Jack—would Tab know what to do about Jack?

She was still lying like that when she heard the parlour door open. She raised her head and glanced round. "Tab—" she began. Then all sound died out of her—the world tilted—for it was at Burke she was gazing. Burke, his hair pasted wetly on his frowning forehead, his eyes fixed upon her as he crossed the shabby, old-fashioned parlour to her. She shrank low in the sofa, but there was no escaping him. His hands came down, found her and pulled her with a certain blindness into his arms. "Don't be frightened of me, Rea," he spoke shakily, humbly. "Oh, my dear, why didn't you tell me Larchmont was blackmailing you? Why did you let me say the things I said to you this afternoon? I'm in hell, remembering—"

"You—you know, Burke?" She touched his face, tentatively, as though to make certain he was real and close to her and saying the things he was saying.

"I know, Rea. Grandfather knows. The whole story, and more, came out tonight, and all the lies are finished with." And swiftly, then, he recounted to her all that had been discovered and said, that night, up at King's Beeches. When the story drew to a close, Burke at last became aware of how lovingly Rea was cradling his neck. Lovingly, her arms sweet and young and close. "Rea, Rea," he whispered, "can you ever forgive me for doubting you? Can you?"

"I could forgive you anything—everything," she said simply. "If you killed me in anger it wouldn't matter, if you did it."

"If I killed you!" The words blurred against her lips. "I love you—love you!" His shaky murmuring died and his lips were warm in the young hollows beneath her cheek-bones, tender against the silken warmth of her throat, ardent and wanting as he found again the trembling gentleness of her mouth. When he finally lifted his head, his sapphire eyes were shimmering, and with his dark, wet hair untidy above them he looked exciting and rakish and slightly dangerous.

"Do—do I know you?" Rea whispered.

Burke gazed down into her eyes, gone drowsy under the storm of kisses. "I'm the man you married," he murmured. "I'd like to be your husband."

"Would you?" She gave a breathless little laugh. "I think that could be arranged, you know."

"Could it really, Rea?" He brushed caressingly at her fair, tumbled fringe; the fringe that made her a child. Yet her eyes, under that fringe, were no longer the child's eyes he remembered. He was half sorry, yet he was also glad, for now he saw that her eyes had become a woman's eyes. "I love you, Rea," he said again, softly. "All the more, I think, because love has been such a long time coming to me."

"But—Burke—there was Dani Larchmont." Rea drew back a little from him, her eyes searching his face. "I thought you loved Dani—there was so much regret in you—and pain—"

"Dani?" His mouth had a sudden wounded look. "Dani was my friend—you are my love. But I hurt Dani, because I couldn't love her. And in her hurt she turned to Philip, and there was nothing there for her but death, when she bore his child."

"Oh, Burke," Rea held him hard, "you couldn't help it, my dear, that you couldn't love her. I expect she knew that, really. She wouldn't want you to go on aching and hurting because of it. I know I shouldn't."

"You!" He spoke into her throat. "You're all heart! I can feel your heart, beating against my mouth. Rea, I'm not too old for you, am I? You once asked to be my daughter—"

"Wasn't I silly?" She smiled and touched the smattering of silver at his temple, a shyness in her, and yet a new self-possession in her as she came to the realization that love turns a girl into a woman, and a man into a boy. "I don't want to be your daughter now. I'm quite grown up now," she said.

"When did you grow up, Rea?" She felt his lips move and she knew he smiled.

"That night we were together in London, I think," she told him. "I—I kissed you, remember? I tried, afterwards, to tell myself I only kissed you because I was grateful for all your lovely presents. But my heart knew differently. My heart ached all that night. Oh, Burke," she clung to him, "Burke darling, I love you so much that I'd never try to keep you from doing the things you really want to do. I'd never try to stop you from going to the ends of the earth, if you want to go. I—I'd never chain you."

"I know that, Rea." Carefully he sat down on the horsehair sofa with her, holding her so that he could watch her face against his arm. "But I'm never going away from you. All my searching has led me to you and I'm content now; the fever to find is quiet." He smiled. "Now I shall settle down to be a thoroughly domesticated English gentleman, adored by you, my cows, and my tenants."

"And little Peter," she said.

"Little Peter!" She felt Burke's arms tighten about her. Then he said: "I want Peter to have King's Beeches, but not if it's going to hurt you. We—we may have a boy of our own."

"A boy who will want to roam the seven seas and all the continents and who must not be stopped by a mere mass of bricks and mortar," Rea whispered.

After that they were quiet and close—until a voice by the door asked whimsically: "Well, my children, how does your garden grow? Have you pulled out all your weeds?"

"Hullo, Tab!" Burke smiled without the least trace of embarrassment as he lifted his face from Rea's hair. "We've ejected the lot—every last one."

"Good!" Tab came to the fireplace and held a spill to the coals. He lit his pipe, puffing strong eddies of smoke into the room. He smiled at Rea and Burke through the smoke. "By the way," he said, "I saw Colonel Mallory this afternoon. He and Iris have decided to go abroad. It seems," Tab's slightly uneven teeth clenched a moment on the stem of his pipe, then they relaxed and he was smiling as he took the pipe from his mouth, "it seems the Colonel fears that another winter in England will riddle him with gout for good and all. They're going to America. The Colonel has a sister there."

"And don't you mind?" Burke watched Tab. "You had a crush on the girl."

"Um, so I did—once." Tab smiled broadly at Rea, curled down in Burke's arms like a kitten with every intention of staying for ever. "You look very much at home," he said. "Tell me, was Jack Larchmont among the weeds?"

"Poor Jack," Rea murmured. "He got so burned—"

"And cleansed by it," Tab added. "Maybe now he'll be the son Jim has always wanted. Who knows?" Suddenly Tab set aside his pipe and walked eagerly to the sideboard. "I think it would be a nice idea if we drank to the future. What do you say?"

"My future rests with Rea, so I'll drink to her," Burke said, and he was watching her. As her mouth curved in involuntary delight at his remark, he bent and kissed her.

Take these 4 best-selling novels FREE
Harlequin Presents
ANNE HAMPSON
gates of steel
Harlequin Presents
ANNE MATHER
sweet revenge
Harlequin Presents
VIOLET WINSPEAR
devil in a silver room
Harlequin Presents
JANET DAILEY
no quarter asked